This book is not for everyone and contains power exchange dynamics. The hero is morally gray and not a warm-and-fuzzy character. Both the hero and heroine are survivors of physical and mental abuse. The hero's father used his religious fervor as a weapon. The book also contains graphic descriptions of sexual activities. If you find any of this objectionable or triggering, stay clear. However, the book is healing and hopeful, and ends with a positive, loving relationship.

My editor, Jason Pettus, for adding some Chicago flavor. Gotta love it.

My cover artist and designer, Consuelo Parra, whose artistry perfectly captures the mood of my novels.

My husband, Barry Wilkins, for his continued support and for listening to my crazy plot ideas. God knows where they come from, and I pray they keep coming.

Lastly, thank you to my dear readers for embracing the first edition of The Devil You Know and making it successful enough for me to return, revise it for this second edition, and continue writing the series it inspired. Thank you.

Where do dark ideas come from? They come from me—Cruz

CONTENTS

I

THE WARLOCK & THE MAIDEN

CRUZ

"What did you say?"

"Nothin', Cruz, nothing," Sophia, my newest acquisition, says as she brings her head up, kneeling in front of me. Red hair masks one side of her face as one panicked brown eye peeks out.

"You know the rules. No speaking unless spoken to, and then yes and no answers. And don't look at me. Understand?"

"Yes, Sir," Sophia says, looking at the stone floor.

Progress: she's acting like a proper sub. Her skin is lit by hundreds of red candles and contrasts with the grey limestone walls of the cellar. The neighbors think it's a wine cellar. Everyone in my neighborhood has one, but it's my dungeon and a perfect one. A home like mine, dating from the 1800s, only comes around once in a lifetime. Luckily, I inherited it. The walls are thick, offering plenty of privacy.

I have a favorite. Doesn't every man? Mine's made of braided red-and-black leather. I remove it from the rack where I keep my copious collection. I caress the handle, run my finger along the thong and popper. I pull Sophia to her feet by the back of her halter and hand her the whip. "Kiss the handle," I order. She takes too long to comply and rolls her eyes, making me swat her to get her attention.

"Ouch, Cruz, you're hurting me," she whines, whirling around. She doesn't know what hurt is. The sting of this whip is awe-inspiring. *I remember well.*

"When I give you an order, you obey quickly," I say. "If I correct you one more time, you won't like the outcome." She lowers her eyes to the floor once more and waits. I have to bring her back to my corner. *I'm letting her get the better of me. Or do I mean the worst?*

Sometimes I'm as close to evil as a person aboveground can be. This could turn into one of those times. I enjoy playing with two girls at once, and Sophia turning on her own even better. Still, Sophia's making me lose my patience, and I don't want that. I want to enjoy them and for them to enjoy me.

In a conspiratorial tone, I point to my other girl, Sadie, tied to the cross. "Start on her ass first, then her back, between her thighs. Vary the strokes, soft and hard. Shoot for ten and watch what you're doing. The idea is to ramp up Sadie's desire and drive her crazy, not break her skin. The safe word is 'gothic.' If she says it, stop what you're doing. If you screw this up, I'll do the same to you."

Sophia strides confidently towards the cross with a slight smile plastered on her face. Sophia shouldn't smile. She'll learn. In a short while, no matter what happens to Sadie, the pain will come back twofold to her. Sophia's like my junkie mother...she couldn't do anything right either. My mother was a whore, and I learned early that most women are. They all want something: drugs, dick, designer shoes. They don't fool me. I make sure they embrace their true nature. They can't hide behind their makeup and pretend smiles. I don't let them. I shine my black mirror on them, unmasking and revealing who they are. Once I do, they become what I want them to be.

I failed once. Her name was River. River had the palest skin, with tiny freckles on her nose. They looked painted on, oh so delicate. I'd never seen freckles on a grown woman before. Pale blue eyes too, and the lightest blonde hair, almost white, the exact color of mine. My right-hand man, Bones, said, "You look like brother and sister." Maybe his telling me that held me back. You don't fuck your sister. I was an only child, a good thing. I wouldn't want anyone, even my worst enemy, to grow up like I did.

River's face was angelic, her expression joyful, and her body cherub-like, round, not angular like mine or my other girls. My house, a converted church, made it seem as if she belonged here, like an angel who had fallen from heaven, hiding with us. The problem was, what to do with her? What would I do with an angel here when I'm no angel myself? Unless I'm Gabriel, the fallen one, and want to clip her wings and bring her to hell on earth?

River had a face that transcended time, ethereal. Or maybe she's a force of nature. I couldn't tell her age. The others insisted she was forty-three, thirteen years older than me. Perhaps her long hair in braids or the too-large clothes she wore to hide her body made her appear younger. You don't know how old a rock or an ocean is by looking either, and her name was River, after all.

The other girls brought her home from the dirty dog (what we call the Greyhound bus station). She lasted almost a year and never succumbed to the evil I had pushed. She said she feared me. *No shit, I'm a scary guy.* But I never brought out the big guns. I never forced her to do anything. Instead, we talked in my library and not about bullshit. I listened to what she thought and felt. She didn't like to disagree with me or anyone, so, more often than not, I reinforced her positions without becoming confrontational. I gave River space to express herself. That's what you do when you have a true submissive. Many of my women go that way, and there are ways you need to handle them. It's not a weakness on their part. It takes strength to surrender to another person. It's not simply them giving up control but handing control to someone they trust implicitly, me. That's a gift I treasure.

River had read the four schools of thought: Idealism, Realism, Pragmatism, and Existentialism. No other bitch in my house or dude in my crew knew what they meant. She spoke languages besides English, too. She could read French and German. She visited the public library almost once a week and brought back piles of books, mostly on philosophy or art history. She was always searching for answers. I could tell she was privileged with her education and manners. Even though her clothes seemed worn, I knew she didn't belong here, so no big surprise when she disappeared. What can you expect? Women aren't trustworthy. My mother, Eddie, proved that.

River's image sneaks into my mind like the vapor of a ghost, clouding it, taking me away from what I should have my mind on: deciding where to open my next house, how many girls I should recruit, why Gia didn't hit her quota last month, and my plan for fucking Sadie and Sophia.

The candles are burning down, and smoke drifts around the room, with the only illumination coming from them. The women, one hung and the other standing, wait for me. Shadows fill the room, making it seem crowded, but even with them here, I'm alone. Scents of cedar and musk permeate the air, and my head hurts again. Time to put this shit to bed (like I ever could) and nail these bitches to mine. "Better the devil you know than the devil you don't," my mother would say under her breath whenever my father left the room.

My father tried to open my mother's eyes and failed. *I won't.*

My mother claimed my father drove her away. A lie. She had a lover—the needle.

Did I drive River away?

Sophia doesn't know me from Adam, but she'll discover she's no Eve tonight. I'm Lucifer, come to life, and I'm going to show her the light. Glory Be!

Swoosh, swoosh, swoosh, swoosh. CRACK.

RIVER

I'm going back. I don't have a choice. I need Cruz's help. Cruz is the only one strong enough and smart enough to take him on. Only if he wants to, but that's the problem—*if.*

The man sitting next to me on the bus keeps taking up more and more space, spreading out. I'm pushed against the window, and his arms are resting near my leg. He brushes against me. An accident? I want to move to another seat, but there's nowhere to go. Passengers are already standing in the aisles, shoulder to shoulder.

Knowing Cruz, he's going to demand something. I can't let him know how desperate I am. But I need to get by Bones, Cruz's gatekeeper, first. I don't have a chance unless he lets me see Cruz. I'll have spent hours on a bus for nothing, and there's no going back.

The man sitting next to me moves his hand to my thigh. *Not an accident.*

"Stop," I call out loud enough for the older woman with the folded walker, sitting on the opposite aisle, to hear. She turns towards us; the overhead light displays her scowl. The man doesn't look at me and moves his hand again, this time between my thighs.

Bones has never liked me since the beginning, because I never earned money or got punished like the others.

"Leave her alone," the woman barks, watching. "If you don't, I'm telling the driver."

Now other people are turning in their seats and watching too.

Cruz doesn't trust women, and it has nothing to do with me leaving. I don't trust men either, so distrust of the opposite sex is something we share.

I remember when Cruz described his father as religious and followed it up with "God-fearing." I couldn't align his father's Baptist beliefs with Cruz's. Why did Cruz choose to practice Wicca and become a witch instead?

Cruz keeps bookshelves full of texts on paganism and the occult. There are altars throughout the house and one in the small garden. He celebrates their holidays and insists all of us are part of his coven, but I never fit in.

I cling to the idea of a higher power and pieces of the Catholic faith I learned in school, but when I was there the last time, I played with some of what Cruz offered. I know when I return to Cruz's house, he'll have a hard time forgiving my betrayal of leaving. Whatever the punishment, I'll deal. I'll do what I have to do to protect myself and them.

My stop is coming up, and I stand. The man's hands move away, and I slide from my seat, holding my backpack. "Thank you," I whisper to the woman who spoke up, and I sprint down the aisle and off the bus into the cold dark.

The exhaust and the bus's squeal as it pulls away make me turn back. I notice the same man from the bus trailing after me. Every time I cross from one street to another, he follows. My heart beats faster and faster as I quicken my pace, the man moving at the same speed I am.

I arrive at Cruz's home in the Hawthorne Place district at midnight. The structure is massive and mostly stone, with church-like spires and arch-shaped entries and windows. Its chimneys, towers, and steeply gabled roof silhouette against a coal-black sky streaked with cobalt blue and an invisible moon. Cruz says the house's style is Gothic, and I agree. As I get closer, I spot the two recent additions, gargoyles and decorative stonework around the windows. The air is frosty and damp even by Chicago's standards. My boots are wet from snow, and my leather gloves are worthless, too thin, and no match for the sleet. The breezes whipping up off Lake Michigan a block away cause me to shiver, and my face is numb to the touch. More sleet blows into my eyes, and diamond flakes stick to my eyelashes as I glance upward. I brush them away and search backward for the man following me, and see his silhouette growing larger.

All the windows in the house are dark, a shame because many of them are stained glass depicting Celtic or religious scenes. Even at night, if the lights are on, you can see them if the blackout shades aren't down. Cruz purchased them to keep the neighbors' prying eyes out. Even in the daytime, the shades are seldom open, because the girls and Cruz sleep during the day, since they often work at night.

I've always loved this house, the place Cruz calls The Palace. It's elegant, with vaulted ceilings in the great room and some bedrooms, fresco paintings, a domed ceiling in the ballroom dining room, squeaky plank flooring, and detailed plaster molding throughout. The property's worth a fortune. The location, one of the best parts of Chicago, plays a role. Cruz only buys, wears, and invests in the best.

"I don't waste time on second-best," he said more than once.

I always question why he let me stay.

We were alone some nights, and after I cleaned the kitchen and the others left for work, Cruz and I talked. We discussed everything. He sought my opinion on books, movies, religion, art, and philosophy. He listened. Cruz has two sides: one frightening, the other comforting. I never understood why, but the scary part never bothered me. I believed he would never hurt me, but maybe I was fooling myself or being naïve. I hope Cruz is in the house tonight to handle the threat I've brought home with me.

I climb the six marble stairs, my heart racing. When I step up, I feel like a child because they've built them for someone tall with long legs, and that's not me. I pause a moment or two, afraid of what will happen when I go inside, even though the man behind me is getting close. I slip and grab hold of the iron railing to keep myself upright. Ice swaddles the steps because no one's put salt out yet. Thankfully, I have a backpack, so my hands are free, and I catch myself holding onto the railing when I slide. The entryway, tall double black doors, face me. Underneath them, greenery fills ornate plaster urns painted red and adorned with twinkling lights. My hand settles on the vegetation, and I paw through frantically. My fingers land on a small metal container buried inside. Bingo—the hide-a-key. I slide the metal covering and hold up the key. The front lanterns kiss the brass before I insert it into the lock and turn. The man crashes into me, causing the door to yank out of my hand, propelling me forward, and the copper skull-shaped knocker to slam.

"Welcome home, River," Cruz says, his hot breath hitting my cheek as he catches me and holds me tight against his chest, looking past me.

2

STAND ON YOUR OWN TWO FEET

CRUZ

Did I conjure River back tonight? She appears even younger than before, if that's possible. Is the fear in her eyes from the asshole behind her, or is she more afraid of me? I let go of her leather-clad hands and push her against the wall of the foyer, out of the stranger's grasp. I recognize a predator when I see one, and grab his throat and squeeze. He's a large man, but I know how to kill people in ways requiring little strength. He struggles to speak as I continue to press on his windpipe, looking deep into his frightened eyes. By now, Bones is by my side.

"Let him go. We don't need the heat," Bones says, and he points back at the row houses of my neighbors, with their windows lit marigold and yellow-white like the color of a Burmese python.

I release the man's throat and toss him out the vestibule, the glass panels lit up by the forged iron lights with cone Tiffany shades.

"I didn't know," the man screams while racing down the steps, slipping and running into the night as my people laugh.

I slam the door and circle River, examining her, and everyone grows quiet. Her clothes are wet, and she wraps her arms around herself, trying to make herself appear smaller. She doesn't look at me. I know what she's up to. Her eyes squeeze close, and she conjures up the invisibility spell she'd bookmarked from my book of spells the last time she was here. She doesn't know that until you accept you're a witch, you can't cast spells, so you remain powerless.

River always got skittish when men got close. Being chased tonight, I'm sure, didn't help matters any. Before she'd left, I believe she'd gotten comfortable with me, even trusting me. She shouldn't. I could destroy her, and it wouldn't take but a day or two. I recognized her fragility instantly when the girls first brought her here. Obviously, the man following saw it too. After spending almost a year with her, I know exactly which buttons to push to bring her to her knees. A pimp sizes up his charges. He figures out which ones are loyal and will do as they're told, which will break rank and need a firmer hand, and which need to go before infecting the herd. The thing is, River never worked for me, not in that way, anyway. I never turned her out; I should have. Each day, I'd decide today would be the day, and then moments later, change my mind, deciding she wasn't ready.

Perhaps I'm wrong about River. Maybe she can cast spells, and she put one on me. In the end, she cost me money. Nothing like this had happened with me before, holding back with another human. I don't like people, but that doesn't mean I won't try, or at least pretend. I love nature, the woods, birds, and animals. I should have realized that my liking of River was a sign.

She peeks at me, her eyes meeting mine, and for a brief instant, an electrical jolt hits me hard. I drag her into the great room by the hand as Bones, two of my crew, and five other girls, including Gia, follow. All are watching intently. I have to do something, or there'd be mutiny.

"River," I say, "go to the table, bend over, and keep your eyes down."

I see the other girls and Bones sneer, but Gia turns away. All but Gia are sick motherfuckers. I've never understood why most people enjoy seeing other people's failures.

River does as I order, placing her delicate hands on either side of one of the narrow oak tables where we break bread.

"Take off your coat, gloves, boots, and hat."

River struggles, stripping them off, the wet leather sticking to her hands and feet. One glove drops on the floor.

"Leave it," I call out as she bends to pick it up.

After she pulls her gray wool cap off, my chest tightens. Her long hair is gone.

She places the hat and one glove on the table, takes a wide stance, and plants her feet.

"What happened to your hair?" I ask.

"I cut it."

"Why?"

"My husband," she says, squeezing her eyes shut.

"Punishment?" I ask.

She nods. "For running the last time." She looks up at me.

Asshole. There are other ways to punish.

"I've got to punish you, too. Tell me why."

"For the same reason. I left without permission," River whispers.

"Say it louder, River."

"I left without permission."

River's voice ricochets off the high ceilings of the great room. I step behind her and box her in. Her hands grip the table harder, and her legs shake.

"There's danger out there," I say, pointing to the door. "And you brought the threat back to my house. What counts appropriate—"

"Give her a hundred," Bones interrupts, tossing me my crop.

"Be quiet, or I'll give you the hundred!" I yell, stepping away from her towards Bones, waving the crop near his face as he dodges my blows. I return and bend closer to River's ear. "How many? Or should I call your stalker and ask his opinion?"

"Please...Cruz, don't. I'm sorry," she says. Her voice soothes me, and her apology makes me want to back off, but I can't, not with the others watching.

"How many?" I ask.

"Twenty," she breathes.

"Twenty sounds right," I say. She knows what she needs. I push down on the hollow of River's back, forcing her torso flat to the table and her ass in the air. "You're to be quiet and not talk back."

"I never talked back," she says. She looks pretty with her short hair and bangs, reminding me of Mia Farrow from *Rosemary's Baby*.

"You don't say," I respond, knowing she hadn't, not in a wrong way, anyway; always funny. I had to work to make her even disagree with me, but when she did...

I rub my hand across her rump, her jeans cold and damp from the weather. The crop will sting, but not as badly as the bullwhip. Luckily for her, the piece is downstairs in the dungeon. I don't make her take her pants off either, which would have caused even more physical torture and mental pain. She's insecure about her body; like so many other women, River thinks she's fat. *I think she's perfect*. I shouldn't keep her waiting. The suspense isn't good for her. She mentioned an anxiety disorder once.

CRACK.

I bring the crop to River's bum with considerable force and keep bringing it down.

She doesn't cry out, not even once. Would the others maintain I hadn't hit her hard enough?

Why do I care what these idiots think?

If anyone dares to say anything, I'll whip them too.

When I'm done, I lead River away from the others to the couch and have Gia bring her ice.

There are no tears or other reactions from River. I would prefer to monitor her, but I leave instead. I can't treat River as special, even though I once imagined she was. She can't tell me where she's been, anyway. Her eyes hold a faraway look...she's somewhere else.

River shouldn't have left to begin with. Disloyal. And to make matters worse, she came back. Yet, my heart is full, and for the first time in a long time, content. River is home.

RIVER

"Spirits of all the people who've died in the house hang out here," Cruz said once. "The ceilings are higher, and there's room to roam." I assumed he was teasing me.

I fall asleep on the couch, and there's a presence. My body floats. First, a man. It's Cruz. A kiss makes my lips burn, then fingers thread through my hair and softly stroke my head. Someone whispers, calling my name.

"Rest. You're safe here. Everything will be alright," and I believe, and he leaves.

Tapping noise. Overwhelming perfume, the stench so overpowering that I hold my breath. A red-haired woman draped in jewels appears. She says I have a purpose. "You have special powers. You can fly, become invisible, and make people soften."

It ends up backfiring. I make Cruz nicer in the dream, and someone stabs and kills him. Startled, I reach out for him, but there's nothing but air. I attempt to get up, but can't move. My head aches, and my chest is heavy. I'm alone in the great room, surrounded by the cold stone walls and the vaulted ceiling with dark wood beams and posts. The walls seem to breathe, moving in and out in time with my own breath. Lesson learned. *Don't change Cruz.* I need Cruz precisely as he is: challenging, unpredictable, with a touch of evil.

I know Cruz won't help me for free. I hear rustling near the couch, but when I turn my head, there's no one. Cruz is going to want something in return. He's wired this way. We discussed it once.

"There are two kinds of people in the world," Cruz once said. "Those who use and abuse and those who get used and abused. Which one am I?" He asked.

I tried to stall and be diplomatic. He prodded me for the truth. "The kind who uses and abuses," I finally confessed.

He smirked at me. "Since you know this, there's no excuse for letting me take advantage of you unless you're a fool, and I know you're not." But I didn't have a choice. I had to come back. I need his help.

More dreams came. My husband's chasing me. He catches and beats me, but that's not the worst part. He locks me in the closet again, like all the times before. It's dark, I'm alone, and I don't know if it's day or night. I'm thirsty and hungry, and I can't help my children. I wake up alone.

3

OFFERINGS

RIVER

I hesitate before bringing my hand to the hardwood, holding it in midair. I check my watch. Cruz doesn't see people until nine. He enjoys solitude and needs more alone time than I or anyone else I know. No one ever bothers him until after he drinks his morning coffee, completes his prayers, and meditates before his altar. *Knock knock*. The sound is louder than I mean it to be, my knuckles tender from bringing my hand down.

Sheila opens the door instead of Cruz. Burning cloves and holly make my eyes water. Cruz burns different herbs and plants to repel evil. I asked him once if his offerings kept him from entering his room. He didn't laugh at my joke and assigned me a list of chores. Sheila is entirely naked except for a black dog collar. Her dark red lips turn up at the corners as she guards the door, blocking me from entering. As much as Cruz needs his downtime, he's always working, training the women, meeting their needs, doing whatever's required to keep his house's businesses operating smoothly. He's not the type to delegate what he believes are essential matters.

Sheila makes me stand there as she smirks, and her eyes travel from the top of my head to my toes, then she rolls them, making me feel inferior and out of my element. The truth is, I am. My body looks nothing like hers. She's tall, and her body is shapely. She has a narrow waist, and her breasts and bum are ample. I'm short and apple-shaped, my stomach's too large, and my chest looks like a boy's. I have nothing to speak of, which explains why my husband gave me a gift certificate for a boob job for Christmas three years back. I never used it, even though my husband never stopped nagging me about it.

My face turns red in embarrassment, seeing Cruz and a naked woman together. Cruz is nothing like anyone I've met before. I've had a crush on him since the first time I stayed. I'm too old to have one, and he's way younger than I am. But somehow, I sense a connection I've never had with anyone else. I realize it's stupid, and most likely it's one-sided. But sometimes, when we used to talk, he'd reveal a different side, and then, like a turtle, he would disappear inside his shell. Cruz's eyes are on me now, not on Sheila.

He's wearing black jeans and no shirt. I watch him turn and grab a white button-down on the chair as I stand in the doorway. He hastily pulls it on, and pieces of his blonde hair fall over his collar. He comes to the door, takes my arm gently, and walks me in. He snatches Sheila's arm like he's going to embrace her, but shoves her into the hallway. Her smile disappears along with her rear end. The last thing I see as I turn around is her horrified expression.

His action toward Sheila surprises me. She's a favorite of his, and as tough as he is, he treats the people who live in the house respectfully.

Cruz looks at me as if examining a species from a faraway planet before speaking.

"Do you always tolerate unacceptable behavior from others? Take off your pants, River." He moves closer to me.

My face heats. "She did nothing. I can't, please." My voice wavers. I want Sheila to come back.

"Do you like it when people look down on you?" Cruz asks.

"Ahh, no, of course not."

"I want to see the damages. Don't disobey."

I can't afford to piss Cruz off when I need his help. Not following his directions will only bring problems and possibly more punishment. Besides expecting the people who live in the house to contribute, Cruz expects each of us to do whatever he commands without question. He doesn't care if people get mad. If you live here, you accept. He's in charge. People seldom leave, except for me, but I had to. I pull down my jeans and underwear far enough to expose my backside. My whole body heats.

Cruz gives a low whistle. "Wow, you bruise easily," he says, running his fingers over my rear. "Good. I iced you, or you would've been worse. Letting you keep your pants on was wise, too. I didn't break your skin. Did anyone ever say you have thin skin? Likely to have trouble sitting for a day or two." He pats me gently. "Keep icing today. You can pull 'em back up." He looks away. I consider Cruz's thin-skinned remark and realize I misinterpreted it. My mother used to say the same thing, but she meant I take what people say to heart too easily.

"How did you sleep after the...." Cruz glances to the end of his bed where the crop lies.

"Restlessly. I think you might be right about the ghosts."

Cruz laughs. "You felt something, did you?"

"It was more than that. I saw a woman with red curly hair, dressed in finery and wearing loads of jewelry." Cruz's expression changes, his eyes becoming dark instead of friendly, forcing me to look away.

Cruz's room is one of the largest in the house, up on the third floor. One wall is stone with a large circle on the floor in front of it; inside the circle is his altar. Across from it is a small alcove. Cruz walks to it, sits in his throne-like chair, crosses his arms, and waits. The chair is black ebony wood, covered with red velvet, and over two hundred years old. He claims it came from France. I imagine Cruz with a gold crown when he takes his seat. There's something regal about him. He carries himself like royalty and doesn't even need the throne or a crown. I wish I could be as confident.

"May I speak with you, please?" I ask.

I'm nervous standing in front of him, and my hands shake. I may be older, but I feel like a child standing here.

"About your visions?" Cruz asks.

"No, something else."

"Sure, talk," he says, staring at me intently. When he meets with anyone, he gives them his undivided attention.

Gia once said, "When I talk with Cruz, he makes me feel like I'm the only one in the world worth paying attention to." I'd prefer he didn't watch me so closely, though. He makes me feel like a tiny bug he might decide to squish at any moment.

I can't help but bounce back and forth on my feet, push my hair behind my ear, and let my eyes wander around the room, landing on the bed again, a four-poster with a tall headboard embellished with acanthus leaves and extravagant carvings of grotesque figures, including the goat man-devil so important around here. Cruz will know I'm nervous, and that's why I'm not looking at him, but the bed makes me nervous too, as I imagine him doing things in it.

Cruz knows all my tells. He once pointed them out to me. He explained to me, "Reading people's body language is an essential skill if you want to be successful. For one example, if they're lying, they blink a lot." When I responded, they might be having trouble with their contacts, Cruz stared right through me and continued, "Or if they're hiding something, their neck and shoulders stiffen. Like yours. Sometimes it's not the body language at all. For instance, people who turn what you say into a joke are deflecting attention from themselves, attempting to ingratiate themselves with you, or they're using their joke to insult you without it appearing that way. Which one, River?"

I didn't provide an answer. I blushed instead, acting like a schoolgirl, saying nothing. I never confessed that the reason I make jokes is that he makes me very nervous because I like him.

His blue eyes are still on me. "Well?" he asks. He needs quiet time, and I've intruded. Cruz doesn't like drama either, and he knows already that I've brought some. He's said more than once, "I like a trouble-free home. A peaceful place. If there's going to be havoc, I'll be the cause, not anyone else."

"I never mentioned it, but I have children," I say. "A son and daughter back in Connecticut. I had to go back."

"You left your children behind? What kind of mother are you?" His lips curl.

"One who's afraid," I say, staring at my feet. Then more words rush out of my mouth. "I left them with my mother the last time, but my husband found them. He threatened to hurt them if I didn't come back. I didn't have a choice. I couldn't leave them with…."

"And?" he asks, bending forward in his chair and tapping his foot. He touches the scar above his right eyebrow. Another tell of Cruz's when he's bored or frustrated. The day I pointed this out, he ended the conversation and didn't speak to me for three days.

"I had to go back. I couldn't put their well-being in jeopardy."

"Why are you back, then?" Cruz asks, his head tilted, one palm open.

"Because he started hurting us again, after promising he wouldn't. This time I brought them with me, but I had nowhere to go. I can't do this alone. I don't know anyone else strong enough or smart enough to take him on and protect us but you."

Cruz laughs. "Are you kidding? I appreciate the compliments, but getting involved with family shit? No, definitely not. It took me years to get away from my own various fucked-up family members. Why would I want to jump into yours?" He crosses his arms, ready to dismiss me.

"I'll do anything if you'll help me. Anything. Please, Cruz." I move closer to him.

He brings his fingertips together. His eyes light up, and a smug expression appears. "Are you offering me your body, River? As tempting as you are, I already have a stable of whores. In fact, several stables. I'm not interested unless I receive every bit of you."

"I'll pay you," I say.

He leans forward and his eyes narrow. "How much? Where will the money come from?"

"As much as you require. I'll get a job," I insist.

"Doing what?" he asks, looking away. "No offense, but you're not cut out for the streets, at least not yet. And working a minimum-wage job to pay me back would take years. Do people with degrees in art history even find positions in that field?"

"I had one once," I say. "I could get one again."

"And I'm supposed to wait?" He closes his eyes for a few seconds. "I might consider a personal arrangement between you and me." His voice becomes gentle, and a relaxed smile appears. Cruz doesn't act like this unless he's preparing to spring a trap. Another of his tells.

"What arrangement?" I ask, on alert.

"Earlier, I mentioned I'm interested in all of you. Body, mind, and soul. Serve me according to my wishes, in whatever capacity I require. You'll become my slave. We can work out the details later. "

"You can't be serious. Slavery isn't legal."

"In my world, it is. If you want my help, that's how it'll be. Now get out." He waves me away. "I have work to do. If you're interested, we can discuss the details tonight. If not, plan to contribute, and you can't live off the rest of us. You work in the kitchen this week, and if we don't work out a deal, you're under Bone's control."

"But Cruz, you haven't heard the rest. I need to bring my children here. I only had enough money to leave them in a hotel for one night, and I can't leave them alone again. I have to go right now and get them."

"You're out of your mind. Kids here? Seriously, River! This isn't a daycare center. You know what we're involved in, even though you never did it." He flashes an evil grin. "You recognize this is not the proper environment for children, right?"

"Cruz, I know I'm asking a lot, but I have nowhere and no one. He's going to come looking, and you don't know what he'll do to get them back. With them gone too, he'll pull out all the stops. And if he gets us back, there'll be no end to the punishment he'll dish out. Please..."

4

DEAL WITH THE DEVIL

CRUZ

BAM BAM. "Who's there?" The unintelligible mumbling identifies the caller. "Bones, get your ass in here!" I yell.

"When can I schedule River with the others?" he asks once he's inside. Bones is Bones because there's no muscle or fat on his six-foot-two-inch frame. Bald too. He's also the whitest person I've ever seen, paler than me, close to being an albino. But if you ask if he is one, he takes offense, and we've been in several bar fights because of it. Grow a spine, I'd like to say to him, but he's the member of my crew who's been with me the longest, and I'll back him up for that reason alone.

"Don't concern yourself for now. I'll let you know what I decide. This time, River's more desperate and willing to deal."

"A deal with the devil?" Bones smiles, his eyes lighting up.

"You know I'm a witch. I'm only evil when I have to be."

"Or when the mood strikes," Bones adds, winking. "Why is she so desperate?"

"Family drama and she's frightened."

"The husband again?" Bones asks. "It ain't good for morale if we don't make her put out. Last time I had a hard time explaining to the others—"

"Shut the fuck up," I say, stalking in front of him. "If you have to explain anything to the girls, you don't have control of them. Do you ever see me explaining anything to them or anyone else? Huh?" I know why he's worried. The last time River worked for *me*. I gave her kitchen and house duties. Not this time.

"Well...no," Bones says, his blue veins throbbing through his pallid skin.

"I've already agreed to help River if she keeps her end of our bargain."

"What bargain's that, Cruz?" Bones asks.

"One between her and me. Get out. And don't bring her up again, ever." Bones' concerns have nothing to do with the girls. Bones wants River. He's wanted her since day one. He continually studies her while licking his lips, and thinks I don't notice. But I notice everything. I noticed Gia wouldn't look at me this morning and didn't do yoga. I noticed no one started the dishwasher last night. I noticed Sheila's eyes jumped with jealousy when River opened the door, and River's self-consciousness when she did.

Bones will never touch River, and neither will any other john. Not happening. Fuck. What's going on with me? River's not even back a day, and I'm treating her like a Vermeer. Her lips last night were as pink and inviting as the model in the painting, the one with the pearls. I couldn't resist them, and when I touched her head, flushed with fever, she mumbled and mentioned spirits and ghosts. Demons, maybe.

The description River gave of her ghost last night was a coincidence, despite fitting Gloria to a T. I was the only spooky apparition at midnight. I placed a blanket over her, sat, and watched over her until her fever disappeared.

Wait until the crew and Bones learn I gave River permission to move her children in. They'll want my head examined. But this time I'll work River, not the other way around. River coming back to me is so much better than me going to hunt her down. I'll even kill for her if circumstances or assholes require it, like the time with Gloria and the one in Brooklyn when someone tried to steal one of my girls.

River agreed to my proposal. Another mistake on her part, like feeding a jellybean to a whale. Whatever River does for me will never be enough. She doesn't know what she's committed to. I check my moon phase app. A new moon, perfect for signing a contract and beginning a new project—training a slave.

RIVER

I knock on the door three times, the signal. Alex, my son, says, "What do you want?" in a deep voice.

"It's Mom, idiot," I say with a laugh. He yanks the door open. The room's a mess. What can I expect when I leave two children alone in a motel? If anything had happened to them...

"Who ya calling an idiot, idiot?" Alex asks as I hug him, and he grapples out of my grasp. He's eleven, going on thirty-one. One of those kids born with an old soul, with no interest in hugs and kisses from his mother.

Joy, my six-year-old daughter, is the opposite. Her name fits her. She bounces off the bed with a coloring book. "Look what I made," she says excitedly, holding the colorful drawing up in the air, bringing it towards my face, and wrapping one arm around my legs.

"Beautiful, baby. I love the colors, especially the pink unicorn. You can bring it to our new place. We're going to my friend Cruz's house. You two are going to share a room for a while, with a TV and your own bathroom. You'll love it." *But will I?*

Alex says with mistrust in his eyes, "We each had our own bedroom, our own bathroom, and a giant house before we came here. I don't want to share a room with a girl."

"If you want to go home, I can take you to the bus station. Your choice. I'm trying to keep you safe with me, but if you don't want that, you're old enough to make your own decision."

"Nah, I want to stay; I'm just sayin' it was different at home. I wish I didn't have to share a room."

"Yes, I understand. It would be better if you had your own. It won't be the same here. In some ways harder and some ways easier." We could try a shelter, but Cruz said shelters were a haven for criminals and not safe for children. Cruz is not a simple guy, but he'll never hit them as their father had. "Promise me you won't contact any of your friends. No one can know where we are. Our secret, understand?"

"Yes," my son says. "You made me leave my phone behind, anyway. How am I going to contact anyone?"

"By using a computer or my phone. Don't. Promise."

"I promise," Alex says.

"Me too," Joy says, smiling, her top tooth missing.

"Alright, get your stuff together. We're going to The Palace."

"Oooh, The Palace! Like in Cinderella!" Joy screams.

"What palace?" Alex asks.

"Cruz's," I say, my heart beating faster and my stomach in knots. Every princess yearns for an enchanted castle and a prince. He's the prince of darkness, I suppose, so one out of two isn't bad. And I'm enchanted by his house, even if it isn't a castle.

"NEVER CALL ATTENTION TO YOURSELF," Cruz said soon after I moved in the first time. "The neighbors don't like noise, and they report suspicious activity to the police. It's very easy; don't be a dumbass, and you won't get caught." I had argued for letting Alex and Joy stay by convincing Cruz that he'd blend in better with his neighbors if he had children in the house. "Yes, nothing more normal than a house filled with a bunch of women and two children," Cruz countered. "Now they'll think I'm a polygamist instead of a pimp."

I use the key Cruz gave me. No one seems to be home. The girls and the rest of the crew are probably out on calls. The girls meet their clients in hotels. Better for everybody, according to Cruz. Only high-end clients who are Cruz's close personal friends visit the house, but only on special occasions, and then it's in the cellar only. A place I've never been.

"Please follow me, sir and lady, and I'll show you to your room," I say, mimicking a British butler, taking Alex and Joy up the grand staircase with curved banisters to their room, the nicest one in the house, usually reserved for the girl with the highest earnings. Cruz uses it as a motivator. No girl has lived in it since Maxine. According to Cruz, she married one of their clients and retired. The room's been empty for eighteen months because Cruz claims no one has earned it yet. He argued with Bones, "Rewarding mediocrity is what's wrong with society. I refuse." Now Alex and Joy will enjoy the high ceilings with frescoes, the wall of arched windows, and the private bathroom and TV. It will raise the hackles of some of the women in the house for sure, but my being a slave will take the edge off for a few.

The children carefully fold their clothes and place them in the dresser, and Joy tucks her toys into the closet and on the nightstand. The few toiletries they put in the bathroom.

Knock knock. "Yes?" I call out. Both children looked up expectantly.

"It's Cruz. I'm coming in."

CRUZ

The littlest one, the girl, a mini-River, runs up, wraps herself around me, and gives me a unicorn drawing. The drawing says, "To Mr. Cruz, Love, Joy." *Shit.* I notice the little girl's arms. They're thin and covered with bruises of different sizes and colors. I used to wear them too, like tattoos. The fire in my belly burns, remembering.

"How did you get those, Cruz?" the teachers used to ask. My parents schooled me on how to answer. *I fell down the steps. I toppled out of a tree. I got a new bike and crashed. I had a nightmare and fell out of bed.* The teachers must have reasoned I was the most uncoordinated kid to ever walk the earth, or maybe they knew exactly what was going on and didn't want to get involved. After all, how do you accuse a chaplain of doing something to his kid? I lived in Ithaca as a child, one of those college towns, the kind you see on calendars and postcards—picture-perfect, with fall foliage and Victorian homes. The outside of things hides the inside. Open the windows and crack the door, and you'll find the ugliness hiding there. Drugs, alcohol, fights, and beatings. No privilege to be found.

I look at the three of them and worry. I already have a family of crooks, misfits, and whores. I don't need a genuine family to bring additional responsibility. Freaky, all of them with light platinum hair, the color of mine. I look at River, and her eyes look moist, like she wants to cry, but she's holding back with everything she's got. What I'm going to do to her is going to cause her more grief and pain, something she's experienced before, but maybe this time—

Ring, Ring. River's face collapses and turns white as she examines the caller ID. She whispers, "My husband, Jack. What should I do?"

I keep my voice low. "Get the call out of the way. Answer and give him the bad news. You ain't coming back. He's not getting them back." I point at the children playing. "Tell him if he goes to the police, you have pictures of the bruises on their bodies and their own testimony. You've hired a law firm. If he wants to be a dick, he can speak with them. Then hang up. Let's go to the hall." I take River's arm and guide her out, closing the door behind us. "You can do this," I say and massage her shoulder.

River presses the answer button and puts her cell on speakerphone. I take my phone out of my pocket and turn on my recording app.

"River, you're going down. It's called kidnapping."

"I, I, I, I... They'll forgive all when they see the bruises you've put there."

"Any marks will be long gone by the time the police see the children, and I have legal custody. After all, you deserted the family the last time. The court will side with me."

"My mother had them until you took them. The children and I will testify, and you'll lose custody."

"The police won't trust you. Someone with a history of drug use?"

"What drug use? I don't do drugs."

"Funny, I found heroin and amphetamines hidden in your nightstand."

"If you did, you planted them."

"Who's going to put faith in you? No one would grant custody to a woman who has left her children before, suffers from depression, and posts pornographic pictures of herself on the internet. If they believe you, they could end up in foster homes."

"What pictures?"

"I'll text a couple."

Pause.

"Oh my God, where did you get these?"

"I drugged you one night and had some fun. Don't worry, I have more of them." *A laugh.* "If you and the kids come home, I'll delete the pics. As I said, with your drug use, depression, and history of abandoning your children, you don't have a chance."

If I'm depressed, you're the cause, and I left Alex and Joy with my mother. I'm not talking anymore. You can discuss all this with my attorney."

"Now, how would you get money to hire an attorney?"

"You're not the only one with friends. I'm not discussing this with you. Anything further, you can send to my attorney."

River hangs up the phone, tears sliding down her face.

"It's like you said, right? He planted the drugs?"

"Yes," she responds, wiping her tears away. "Could they really end up in foster care? And what about the pictures?"

"Not likely. He's running scared. I have his threats on tape. What's the big deal over a couple of pictures?"

"What if my children see the pictures someday?"

I shake my head, not bothering to answer. "What's this guy's name?"

"Jack Pearson."

I can't control myself, and chuckles pour out. I stare at the ceiling. "Jack Pearson, the real estate tycoon? You're his wife?"

"I wouldn't describe him exactly like that, but yes."

"You left a life of wealth and comfort to—"

"He had money, not me. There's a cost to everything. He gave me something valuable, my children, but now he wants to take them away."

"I would've preferred to know who I'd be going up against before I agreed to this. Your husband's got powerful friends. The Russian mafia, for one."

"You can change your mind," she mumbles, her eyes getting a faraway look.

"We don't need your help anyway," River's son Alex suddenly says, peeking out the doorway, his eyes angry. "I can protect us fine."

"I'm sure you can, boy, but don't you know you shouldn't snoop?" I turn to River. "A promise is a promise. Come to my office in half an hour, so we can work out the other matter. And those pictures, they're of no consequence. Anything he puts up, I can take down. How do you think I've kept my reputation so squeaky clean?"

5

CROOKS, MISFITS & WHORES

CRUZ

I look at my watch after the soft knock. River's right on time. I almost didn't hear it. She probably doesn't want me to. I open the door, and she glances up with a sick expression. "I don't know if I can do this," she says with a pale face. "I've never done something like this before." Her eyes dart back and forth.

"Of course you haven't," I say, grabbing her arm, escorting her in, and guiding her to my desk.

Her eyes fall over it. "I've never seen this before."

"It just got delivered. It's French 19th-century Revival, Hunt style. Notice the foxhead drawers." I point them out to her. "I purchased it at auction."

"I love the legs. Barely twisted columns. And the leather inserts on the top surface," she says. "Is it made of oak?" Her eyes drift over it.

"Yes. Now, back to the other issue. I realize this is all new to you, but our relationship will now be based on mutual respect. I can't do anything I want with you...Well, I take it back. I can." I laugh. "But I need your consent. Read the contract before falling apart. If there's something totally objectionable, we can negotiate. But I warn you, I'm not negotiating everything." I remove the document from the drawer, place it on the desk, and shove the stapled papers toward her. "Understand?"

"Yes," she says, sitting down, stretching for the document, handling the edges like an object trip-wired to explode.

The last time she was here, River turned the tables on me a few times in conversations, taking what I'd said and using my words against me. I found it surprising because River's tendency is to please. She agrees most of the time, even when she's in the right, but you never know; there might be a fire underneath. I hope River surprises me and tries to negotiate some of this.

Her eyes race across the lines, stopping here and there. Her face changes while reading each section; sometimes her lips slant downwards, while other times her eyes open wide. Once a tear even appears, she wipes it away. The problem with having slaves is that, as much work as it takes to make someone a slave, it takes just as much to undo. Some individuals find comfort in being under someone else's control. When they aren't anymore, they lose the very foundation of their lives. "The floor becomes Jell-O, so to speak," Gloria once said. "Much easier to find a new Master to take them off your hands, and you tire of them." She tried it with me. I push the thought down, my stomach tightening. I prefer the alpha submissive type. Much more of a challenge, and a sense of accomplishment when done. I muse about which way River will fall.

Finally, she flips to the fourth page, and when she arrives at the bottom, she places the paper face down on the table and closes her eyes like she doesn't want to see.

"Essentially, I belong to you," she says, speaking to her chest. "I'm to wait on you as desired and carry out all household and personal duties you require. I'm not allowed to read, write, watch television or use a computer unless you say so. I'm to address you as Master or Sir, and my name is 'Slave' or 'Seven.' If I disrespect you, you'll punish me. I'm to dress only in what you give me to wear or nothing, and only eat food you direct me to consume when you grant permission. I will not argue or complain. I'm not to speak unless spoken to. You can use me any way you want, as a sexual plaything for yourself or for others. I'm unsure I understand the one section on orgasm denial." Her face turns red, and her eyes drift up to mine.

"What don't you understand? You're not to have an orgasm unless I say you can." I'm surprised she'd have an issue with this part when so many others could cause her more problems.

"I seldom have sex, and when I do, it takes a long time to have one. I've only had two in my entire life." Her hands part in front of her, palms up. "Trying not to have an orgasm sounds counterproductive."

"What a pity. Married twice and only two orgasms in your life?" I choke back a chuckle. "I appreciate your honesty. You present a good argument, since you've practiced it so much in the past, but I'm sure the way I'd do it with you would be different. I agree to delete that portion and teach you how to have orgasms and increase your count. I have tools and toys to help."

River's face turns red, and she turns back to the desk. "And the part about having sex with other people…"

"Yes?"

"I'm not comfortable having sex with others."

"Nor should you be, unless you're a skag, and I don't believe you are. At least you weren't the last time you were here. Simply a test of your loyalty to me. I'm not saying I'd give you to Bones." Her face turns white, and she stares at me. "I'm kidding. If I made you go with someone else, we'd discuss the person and what the sexual act would involve, and you'd have to consent." I slap the table. "I'd like this section to remain as written. Do you agree?"

River closes her eyes. "I suppose I have to, since you gave in on the previous one. Why can't I use my real name? And why 'Seven?'"

"I knew you'd catch that. You're the seventh slave I've had. River won't exist once you sign the contract."

Her expression darkens, and she brings her eyes to the desk again. "What will my children think if you call me Slave?"

"Simple. If I'm with you and your children, I'll call you Seven. Tell them it's a nickname."

"What does this mean?" she asks, pointing at the safe word section.

"You say the word 'gothic' to bring everything going on to a halt if you feel overwhelmed or in danger."

Her eyes panic for an instant, and her mouth drops open. "There's no end date in this," she says, a wrinkle appearing above her nose.

"No, I kept the contract open. We'll both sign today, and I'll collar you tonight. We'll do this for a week, then come back and revise the contract to suit both of us. We can come back to it every month and tweak it. You can plan on a minimum of a year's service unless I end early or you have a nervous breakdown." I smile at her. "You read the part that says all the rooms have cameras?"

"I remember that from before. I don't feel comfortable without a completion date. The maximum should be one year, not the minimum."

"So be it. A one-year termination unless I choose to end early." Most likely, I would tire of her well before then. "Did you read the punishment part?"

"Yes. Would you do all those things listed?" River asks, her eyes watering as she stands up.

"I have in the past, but truthfully, some were idiots, and I know you'll be perfect. I can't imagine hurting you." I seize her hand, her fingers stiffening. "If I didn't like you, you'd be with Bones already." I stroke her hand as her body trembles.

"Promise me you won't be mean on purpose," River says, staring up at me, her blue eyes trusting.

"Have you ever seen me be mean on purpose?"

"Yes."

I'm surprised by River's honesty. She never liked to hurt people. The first time she was here, she avoided conflict of any sort. "I promise, I won't be mean on purpose." I could never make the promise to anyone else, but with River, I can keep such an oath. "Before you leave, you need to sign the contract. And one more thing—we need to discuss your limits, things you're not willing to do."

"Ah...I don't know."

"Think, River. If you put nothing on here, I can do whatever I want to you."

"Um, I really don't know," she says, swallowing.

"Fine, we'll come back to it in a week. By then, you might have some thoughts for this section." I hand her the pen and then notice her wrist. "I forgot, hand over your watch. You don't need it. You're on my time now."

After she signs, I feel euphoria, then unease. I want to possess her and protect her from anyone who would do her harm. I chastise myself for caring as I toss her watch into the desk drawer.

***

We sit in the ballroom, which most of the time serves as our dining room. River sits on my right, Bones to my left. My crew sits around the rest of my table. My sex workers, at least those not working this evening, sit at the other two tables. I have the children eat dinner in the kitchen with my more maternal workers; the older ones have more affinity for children. Quite a few profess a desire to spend time with Joy and Alex once they learn there are kids in the house.

I make my big announcement after dinner. I move to the middle of the room. "Attention. We have a new slave in The Palace." Everyone turns and stares at River. Her pale skin turns pink, and her head goes to the floor. "Stand, River, and come." Whether she knows it or not, she does it perfectly. Her embarrassment makes her keep her eyes on the floor. "Kneel." I help her to the hardwood, take the collar out of my pocket, and buckle the leather around her neck. An artery in her neck moves, and I fight the urge to place bites and kisses all over her throat, but somehow I do. For now, only a simple leather training collar. I'll give her the platinum one with the tiny lock, one of Gloria's favorites, if she pleases me.

"Rise." I present my hand and assist River to her feet. "River is now my slave. You will refer to her as Seven. Note the word '*my*.' You are not to order Seven around. If you want her services, you are to ask me, and I will decide whether they are worth taking time away from me. Be aware that there are now two children staying here: Seven's son, Alex, and daughter, Joy. Please be conscious and watch your behavior and language when they are present. If you do anything that negatively affects their young minds, I will trounce you. Do I make myself clear?" I look around at everyone who remains in silence. "Questions? None? Perfect. Let's celebrate with champagne and dessert."

I escort River back to the table. "Protocol requires you to thank your Master for their collar, slave."

"Thank you, Master," River mumbles as I sit. I want her to talk back so I can punish her, not go along with me.

"Stand by my side," I direct. Dessert comes, and everyone waits for me to take a bite before they eat theirs. I pick up my fork and dig in, and the rest begin eating. I motion to River. "Sit on my lap."

River hesitates, searching the room for help. "I'm too heavy," she says, her face red.

"Do it," I say. After River sits, I bring a forkful of cake to her mouth. She turns her face away. "River, eat." All the men at the table watch as she refuses.

"Please, I don't want the cake. I'm fat enough."

She mentioned once that tiramisu was her favorite. Now she's disobeying me in front of my men over a piece of cake. I'm pissed. "Take a bite," I say, my rage simmering, a headache forming.

She shakes her head and tries to leave my lap. I hold her hand, keep her in place, grind my teeth, then pull her down. Her ass hits my lap, crushing my balls, the pain enraging me further. "You don't leave the table without asking permission, slave. In fact, you don't move unless I tell you to. Understand?"

"Can I leave, please?"

"No. It's 'Master, can I please leave the table' or 'Master, is there any way I can serve you before leaving the table?'"

"Master, can I please leave the table?"

"No. You can kneel by my side and consider all the ways you screwed up and how you're going to correct them going forward. First rule: never disparage yourself in front of me. If there's something to correct, I'll point it out to you." Everyone watches me bring River to her knees. Eventually, they leave the table, and I do too. I kept River there for over an hour. Even the kitchen cleanup crew is gone when I return, and Alex and Joy show up, thinking their mother's playing a game.

I intercede. "Attend to your children, and when you're done, come to my room." River's eyes register relief, shining at me as she stumbles to her feet.

6

TOO FAR, TOO FAST

CRUZ

nock, knock. "Come in," I yell.

River opens the door, and as soon as she spots Melinda's ass in the air, her eyes grow huge, her cheeks turn pink, and she backs out of the room.

"Don't move," I call out, making them both freeze in place as I work the butt plug into Melinda. "Come in, Seven, and close the door. From now on, when you enter, don't knock. Even if I have another woman in here, like now, you're my slave, so this is of no consequence to you, them or me. Consider yourself a piece of furniture. Essentially, you don't exist unless I want you to. If I want to have sex in front of you, I will."

River says nothing.

I add, "The correct response is 'Yes, Master.'"

"Yes, Master," River says, standing by the closed door as I work on Melinda.

I have a ritual most evenings. Each girl who works for me stops by my room. They discuss their day and concerns. I ensure each one gets attention and feels cared for, either here or in the cellar if she needs a more extended session. Melinda is the last one on tonight's schedule. She said she was feeling down, and I will change that. Melinda enjoys being watched when she has sex, so River's showing up is perfect. Ever since River's arrival, I've felt Melinda's excitement growing. She pushes against the butt plug, letting the toy slide in deeper. I turn on a small vibrator with my other hand and slide the piece under Melinda's body onto her clit as she thrashes.

"Has someone ever fucked you in the ass, River?" I ask. The room is quiet except for the whir of the vibrator and Melinda's soft moans. "I asked a question. I expect an answer, slave."

"Do you mean literally or figuratively?" River asks softly.

"Like this," I say. River's nervous if she's using humor in her answer. "Come over here and get a closer look." Melinda gasps and takes even more of the larger butt plug in her ass. Another push, and it's fully in. I wait a few moments, then grab the plug and begin sliding it out and back in again. A minute or two of this, and she'll be more than ready to accommodate me if I want.

River is four feet away now. I motion for her to come to my side.

"Kneel and unzip my pants."

River fumbles with the zipper.

"Be careful, Seven. I like to spill blood, but not mine." I grin. "Open a condom and hand it to me." I motion to the top of my nightstand.

River wrestles with the condom packaging like she's solving a Rubik's Cube. Tired of waiting, I snatch and rip open the packet myself, roll the sheath over my cock.

"Haven't you ever helped your husband with this before?"

"No. My husband doesn't wear one. I can't have more children."

I bring my cock to Melinda's ass. Having River watch me

with Melinda has given me a harder erection than I'd normally have. Initially, I'd only planned to use the plug and vibrator to bring Melinda off, but with River here, I want to go further. I slowly remove the butt plug from Melinda's ass as she fights to hold onto it. I work the head of my cock into Melinda as she struggles.

"River, get the other vibrator on the nightstand, the long pink one, and turn it on." After she returns, I say, "Place it in Melinda's pussy."

"I...I can't," River whispers, her hands shaking.

I open my hand, taking the toy from River.

"Having this will make things less painful for her. She'll be in a more relaxed state and can receive me more easily."

I slide the vibrating dildo underneath Melinda and push it into her pussy. After that, things improve. Melinda's ass bucks back as I thrust more of my cock in. Eventually, she takes all of me. I wanted to see how far I could push both of them when they're together. Now I know. I can't get River far at all, while Melinda will go further.

I glance at River. She looks away and closes her eyes. "Open your eyes and watch, Seven. I want you to see how much Melinda's enjoying this." River's eyes move to the side of Melinda's face and study her as Melinda continues to buck back against my cock and positions her ass higher in the air, capturing me as I slide in and out of her.

I can't last much longer, and neither can Melinda, not with a vibrator on her clit, another in her pussy, and me fucking her ass. And River watching is making Melinda and me even more excited.

"Hold Melinda's hand, River," I say, and they extend their hands, grasping each other.

Part of Melinda's kink is having others watch and touch her during the sex act. Melinda gives out a long, guttural groan. I reach over and stroke River's head to signal my appreciation of her efforts to please me and serve Melinda. River's silky hair parts through my fingers.

Seconds later, Melinda's ass constricts around my cock, squeezing me even tighter.

"Oh *God*," Melinda screams, giving in to her orgasm.

I let myself go too, shooting my load into Melinda while fingering River's hair and watching the side of her face flush. River looks so beautiful.

After Melinda milks the last bit of cum from my cock, I pull myself and the vibrators out of her and hand the toys to a shocked River.

"Slave, take them to the sink, get a warm washcloth, and come back."

After she returns, I say, "Clean me with the washcloth," holding my flaccid cock up for her. River blushes, and after she wipes me off gently, I point to the bed.

"Clean Melinda, too."

River's face turns redder. "I...I can't."

"You can." I guide River's hand, holding the cloth between Melinda's legs, and remove my hand, watching River stand there. "Do it," I say. When River doesn't move, I take the cloth and clean Melinda myself. "Take the cloth back to the bathroom and clean the toys, River. Use soap and hot water, and then alcohol."

I bring Melinda to her feet and hand her the robe. "Are you better now?" I ask.

"Fantastic, Cruz. I had fun." She kisses my cheek and turns to leave. I slap her ass and open the door as she looks towards the bathroom with a grin.

Minutes later, River returns from the other room. "What happened to not being mean?" she asks softly, placing the toys on the nightstand.

I stride towards her, looming menacingly. "Are you judging your Master?"

"No, but since I've agreed to this, all you've done is yell and try your best to humiliate me. I can't please you, no matter what I do, and now this." She motions towards the bed.

"You do please me. And what do you mean, 'try my best to humiliate you?' Am I not doing a good enough job as your Master, slave?"

River says nothing. "Go to my chair and kneel." After she's in place, I sit in my chair and stare at her. "You learn through correction. As far as this goes," pointing back to the bed, "I provided instruction in an area you're sorely lacking in. You have much to learn. I give to you according to your needs."

River doesn't respond, and I keep my eyes on her face. Her eyes are wet. I can see that I need to back off for the moment. I need to offer her some reassurance.

"It's normal to have an adjustment period," I say.

"There's nothing normal about any of this. I can't do this. I lived on pins and needles back at home, attempting to please my second husband. I can't live my life dependent on pleasing others."

"If you want to keep them safe, you'd better," I growl, nodding my head to the room next door where her children are staying. I instantly regret it. I would never hurt them.

River's eyes grow angry and defiant. "My husband, Jack, used to say those exact words. He blackmailed me to keep them safe. I'm sorry, Cruz. This was a mistake. I didn't realize you'd act differently than you did before." She gets up off the floor, unfastens the collar, and holds out the leather ribbon. "We can leave now or in the morning, whichever you prefer."

"Why don't you reflect more, Seven," I respond, refusing to accept it from her. "Come back in the morning and let me know your plans. If there was something that happened beyond what you can tolerate, we can discuss it during your free period, and if need be, add it to your limits list at the end of the week."

River says nothing more and leaves my room, closing the door behind her.

Christ. My head's killing me...another migraine.

***

"Where is she, Cruz?" Gia asks.

"In her children's room," I say, pointing at the monitor on my bookshelf. We watch River lie down on the floor between the two twin beds where her children are sleeping.

"She's not sleeping with you?" Gia leans in, moving closer.

"She insisted on leaving. I wanted to reassure her, but—"

"She's never been a sub before," Gia sighs. "She has no experience with any of this. The first few days of being a slave are tough."

"You remember it, Six?" I reach out and hold Gia's hand.

"Of course. I'll never forget. I was terrified. But I learned so much about myself. I've never regretted it."

"Me too..." I'd almost disclosed something I hadn't meant to. "I mean, being responsible for someone is scary."

"Yes, Cruz. I wonder how you do it sometimes. Being responsible for all of us."

Then my thoughts return to River. "I'm concerned her experience with her husband may make things harder."

"Yes, memories of past events can complicate matters. But it can be cathartic too, and eventually they'll all fade away, because her thoughts will be of only you."

"I had to come down hard to prove to others and River I'm serious about this."

"I don't think you need to worry. Melinda is already telling everyone. Do you think it's possible River will leave?"

"Not likely. Her goal of keeping her children safe overrides any other concerns for herself. That said, I might have moved too far, too fast here. I'm counting on you, Gia, to keep an eye out. River will need a shoulder to cry on. You're someone who can share her experience."

"Yes, no problem, Cruz. You can count on me." She gives me a kiss and leaves the room.

I see movement on the monitor and move closer to watch.

7

SKULL & BUTTERFLY

RIVER

I lay on my children's floor while they sleep, replaying the scene, making me wet. I run my hand across my pussy, up and down, imagining my fingers are Cruz's—

Buzz buzz. A text message. I bring my hands to the side of my body, wipe my hands on my panties, pick up my cell and see his text.

Stop touching yourself.

?

Contract states no masturbation without permission

If you continue, handcuffs.

. . .

OMG. Cruz caught me. My whole body shudders. I lock my knees together. I reach for my blanket. I'm in a cold sweat. There are no accidents in Cruz's world. I'd seen him play games with the others the last time I stayed here, to teach a lesson, send a warning, or give a reward, but he'd done nothing to me until tonight. I'd always viewed his games as harmless. I stare at the ceiling.

He'd made me a part of his sex act with Melinda, killing two birds with one stone. Or was it three?

Cruz fulfilled Melinda's desire, tore down my defenses, and showed to the house my slave contract is real. Melinda would most likely spread the word.

I'd made a mistake coming here. The saving grace is that my children are asleep and safe, and no one can hurt them.

Buzz buzz.

Is he kidding me? Leave me alone. I pick up my cell again and get another text. It's not Cruz.

> U really think I'm going 2 let u take them?

> No way in hell

> I know ur in Chicago

I ignore my husband's taunts and power off the phone. My body shakes, and not from desire. I can't leave Cruz's protection. All he's demanding is my obedience and submission, and I gave both to my husband for eleven years. What's one year with Cruz to ensure the safety of my children?

I hold the collar in my hand. The leather is soft. Unfortunately, when wrapped around my neck, it isn't. The collar's a constant reminder: I'm not in control, and even if I leave here, I won't be. I yearn for a time I won't be under someone's thumb, but tonight, in Cruz's room, being under Cruz's control excited me. Each move he made held an element of surprise. He pushed me out of my comfort zone, and by the end, I was in a frenzy, my body in need.

I always wondered how a man's cock could fit into a woman's tiny rear. Now I know there's a process to anal sex. Initially, the idea made me cringe, but Melinda seemed to love what Cruz did and went along willingly. The three of us, at one point, connected; Cruz fucking her while touching me, me squeezing Melinda's fingers. It's hard to explain or admit to myself, but I enjoyed bearing witness to Melinda's orgasm. When her shuddering traveled through my fingertips, a burning pain seared my heart—jealousy.

I ponder what Cruz might have done that he's had to wipe it clean off the internet. I think about what happened, what may happen in the future, and what I can do about it, getting lost in the plaster designs on the ceiling. I struggle to sleep, but it doesn't come until dawn.

Bam bam. "Yes…umm. Who's there?" I call out, crawling from the floor.

"Bones."

"Just a moment," I argue with myself. Should I open the door for him? I look back at my children's beds. Thankfully, Alex and Joy are still asleep. I glance towards the windows; a little sunlight filters through the blackout shades. I don't remember closing them. I hesitate before opening the door. Bones stares at me, head tilted to one side, and leans closer. "Why aren't you in Cruz's room with him?"

"None of your business," a voice calls out. Cruz takes wide

steps towards Bones from behind him, his chest out and eyes angry.

Bones backs away from my door and Cruz. "I was just check—" he begins.

"Unless I ask you to check on her or the children, you keep away from them." His stare is direct, and there's no warmth. "Understand?"

"Got it," Bones says, hurrying away.

"Are you ready to talk?" Cruz asks as he moves towards the collar in my hands and then pulls back.

I follow Cruz into his room and hand him the collar. "I've changed my mind," I say.

"You need to do better than that, Seven," he says, sitting down in his chair and grimacing, crossing his arms. Colors dance on the floor and fall over him from the stained-glass transept window running the room's length, while the enormous windows on either side of the bed remain closed.

"I apologize, Master. I know I was a disappointment last night."

"You were, but if you'd have stayed, we could've worked out our differences. Running isn't the answer." He bends forward and touches the side of my face. "You don't have to answer questions from Bones or anyone else unless I tell you to. If they have questions, send them to me."

Ahh. "Thank you."

Cruz drinks his coffee. "Sit on the floor," he says. "Explain what you meant when you said you didn't want to repeat 'being on pins and needles trying to please someone.'" Cruz appears totally relaxed, unlike me. He's wearing cargo pants, tall boots, and a black leather vest. I can see his tribal tattoos running up his toned arms. He has large hands with long fingers and wears several big silver rings on his right hand. One I remember from last time: a giant skull with butterfly wings floating atop it, which he wears on his index finger. The smell of sandalwood and spring grass permeates the air. I'm still wearing my clothes from yesterday, rumpled, and my hair is a mess compared to his.

I stare at the ring and answer. "If I displeased him, he would blow up, berate, and…beat me. I was never adequate. Something was always wrong with me. Sometimes he went after the children, too. My mother told me not to marry him. She said it was too soon after my first husband died. I should have listened."

"You admire the ring, River?" Cruz asks, noticing my staring and bringing his hand closer. "Do you know what it means?"

"That a butterfly starts as a caterpillar and grows, eventually into something beautiful."

"A start. I thought you said you studied art history."

"I did. I love the subject."

"This is designed to invoke the feel of *vanitas* paintings," he says.

"Yes…moral lessons, a reminder that our time on earth is not infinite."

"The skull represents our mortality, and the butterfly symbolizes transformation, spirituality, and individuality. The ability of a butterfly to transform suggests we embrace change as well, then spread our wings and fly."

In the spirit of it, I say, "Even the metal itself, white gold, is a reminder. You can't take your wealth with you."

"Platinum too." He pauses. "How did your mother die?"

"How do you know she's dead?" I ask in shock. I hadn't mentioned it to Cruz at all.

"If she wasn't, you would have gone to her for help."

"Suicide. I was the one who found her, hanging in her bedroom closet."

Cruz is slick; he always knows how to get answers out of people. One reason he knows everything about everybody in his house. I stare back at the ring after he gives no reaction to my mother's death. Most people fall apart, apologize for asking, and mutter how sorry they are until you become embarrassed and lie, telling them you're over it. Even though you never will be. I still see her body hanging, the blue face with bulging eyes, the rope cutting into her neck. I push all the wonderful memories of my mother away because of the other image seared into my mind forever.

"Do you suspect I'm going to hurt you, River?"

"My husband beat me. And you hit me with a crop the other night."

He looks away from me like he's sorry, but I'm probably reading too much into it. I've never seen Cruz feel bad over anything, and I often agree with his actions. He maintains order in the house and keeps us safe.

"I'm used to getting hit, and to be honest, your beating wasn't bad. But you can hurt people with words worse. What hurts most is the humiliation, the way you called me out and punished me in front of the others."

Cruz beams. "So I'm successful at humiliating you after all. Is this what you're telling me, Seven?"

"Yes. I'm in a difficult position. Punishing me in front of everyone like you did last night was horrible. But I need your help, and there isn't another way to get it." I hand him the collar and kneel before him. "I'll be your slave, but please, Cruz, I beg you, save your cruelty for my husband."

"Slaves don't ask for anything," he says, letting out a long sigh with his hands in his lap, holding the collar. "Although I'm looking forward to handling your husband. Did you consider he might have killed your mother, or had her killed?"

My knees buckle, and the room spins.

"I—I'mmm not sure."

I never had until now. She suffered from severe arthritis.

"It had depressed my mother when he tried to hurt the children. She didn't leave a note and had never mentioned the desire to kill herself."

"You suffer from depression, too, correct?" Cruz asks.

"Wouldn't you, if someone controlled your every move and hurt you?"

Cruz closes his eyes as if processing what I'm saying. "What do you theorize I'm going to do? Do you think you're up to it?"

"I don't know, but hopefully you'll treat me better than my husband."

"Slaves accept what their Masters give them, believing their Masters know best. In my experience, the thing a slave fears most is what they most need." Cruz wraps the leather collar around my neck, looks into my eyes, and holds the ends expectantly.

"I pray, Master, you want what's best for my children."

"I can't argue with that," he says and fastens the buckle, the collar now tightly bound around my neck. "Try to follow the rules, Seven. Be ready to please. 'Yes, Master,' 'no, Master' in response to questions, and keep your head bowed in my presence. Don't look me in the eye unless I give you permission, and don't become argumentative."

"Can I ask a question, Master?"

"I'll answer one. But in the future, write your list of questions in advance and give them to me, and I'll decide which ones are important and that I wish to answer. You can also save questions for your free period, when I'll allow you to express yourself freely. What's the question?"

"Why does Bones seem to dislike me?"

Cruz laughs at me and shakes his head. "The opposite, River. You're smart. Think."

"Because you didn't make me go out with the others the last time I was here?"

"A good guess. But don't you notice the way he looks at you all the time?"

"No. Sometimes he scowls at me."

Laughing. "No, he's attracted to you."

"No," I scoff.

Cruz's face changes; he loses his smile. "Are you arguing with your Master?"

"No, Master, but why would Bones be interested in me?"

"Why wouldn't he? Is there something wrong with you?"

"I don't look like the others. They're sophisticated and shapely, and my body's... I'm flat like a boy, and I'm fat. Plus, I'm older than all the others."

"Chronologically older, but not in other ways. Let's see your body. Take your clothes off."

"What?"

"I don't enjoy repeating myself. Do it. I should have done this yesterday, inspected my property."

"Property?"

"You belong to me now. You agreed and signed the slave contract. Therefore, you're my property." He pauses. "I'm waiting. Take your clothes off and don't look at me." Cruz looks at his hands and then back at me like he's bored.

"You take yours off first," I say. As soon as the words pop out, I realize I've made a mistake.

8

HUSBANDS, BOYFRIENDS, GIRLFRIENDS, ME?

CRUZ

"That's not how this works," Cruz says gruffly. "I realize you're nervous, but don't talk back again. You don't call the shots, I do. Undress."

My whole body heats. Am I going to faint? Should I refuse or run? Everything seems in slow motion. I pull the long-sleeved T-shirt over my head and cover my chest with the balled-up garment. I don't want Cruz to see.

"Fold your clothes and put them on the bookcase, and then come back over here and stand."

"My underclothes too?" I stand by the bookcase, clumsy and exposed.

"Of course," Cruz says. It sounds crazy, having been married twice, but I've never stood completely naked in front of someone before, at least not like this. Does Cruz think he's made a mistake? I peek, lifting my eyes from the floor. Cruz's eyes travel over my body as his hand slips inside his undone zipper, grabs his cock, and strokes himself. I watch his eyes, and they crinkle at the edges. I know deep within that he likes what he sees. I don't feel weak anymore, but just the opposite, powerful.

"I know you think you want to leave, but the truth is, you don't," Cruz says. "You're safer with me than you will ever be with another. Sit on my lap." He motions me over.

I want to scream no, but don't. I see Cruz's eyes grow larger as I sashay toward him. I lower myself down, not looking at his face. I wonder if he thinks I weigh too much when I land. Jack said I was fat, but I've had two children, so what does he expect? My mind goes in circles. What does Cruz think about my stomach and my chest? I can feel his penis throbbing against my butt cheeks. I push his hand away and take over, wrapping my hand around the base and bringing it up the length of his cock. He sighs. "No can do, slave. If I wanted that, I would have asked. You do nothing unless I tell you to. If you're honest with yourself, you're doing this to distract me, because you're uncomfortable."

My face reddens, and I take my hand away. *He's right.*

"What are those marks on your back?" Cruz asks, brushing his fingers gently against them. His touch makes me imagine a bird's wings fluttering, flying past me.

"Nothing, Master."

"Nothing, huh? Looks like scars to me. And what about these bruises? Tell me the truth, slave."

"No," I say. Cruz knows too much already. It makes little sense to provide additional information he can use against me.

"Did you tell me no?"

"Yes," I lift my head to see how he's taking it.

Cruz stares at me like he's going to light me on fire. "It's 'yes, Master,'" he says. I bring my eyes to my lap.

Minutes pass, and his hands travel to other places: my neck, my arms, my hips. My heart beats faster and faster as I sit on his knees. He wraps his hands around my waist, capturing me. It's the closest I've ever been to him. Is he mad about my disobedience?

"I like the way you feel, Seven." Cruz moves back and looks at me. "I apologize for rushing you last night. Disregarding your feelings, making you feel like an object. I should have moved more slowly."

"Only I can make myself feel bad," I say. "I'm responsible for my feelings, not you."

He rolls his eyes. "I don't know what to do with you."

"Really? Can I get off your lap, then?" I ask.

Cruz coughs, clears his throat. "You're not a suitable slave and...."

"Is it my body?" I ask, my confidence sinking after he pushed my hand away from him, and now the word...suitable.

"Hush. Don't be ridiculous." He strokes my breasts. "I approve of your body. In fact, it's lovely. You're not boy-like at all." He captures a breast in his hand, squeezes, then does the same to the other, examining them. Finally, he pinches each nipple, then bends his head and buries it between my breasts. His breath is hot on my skin, and his tongue travels to my nipples and swirls around them, making me gasp. He moves on to the other one and continues to lick and suck, going back and forth until my nipples are as red and hard as pebbles, and my body hums. "Very nice," he says, then he moves his hand to my inner thighs and strokes each, bringing his hand closer and closer until I—

"What are you doing? I didn't tell you to leave my lap," he says, yanking me back and making me reach for his shoulders to balance myself.

"I should check on Alex and Joy." I shift on his lap.

"Not until I'm done with you. I control every aspect of your life now. You only move when I release you. Understand?"

"Yes, Master, but my children…" I plead, still holding his shoulders.

"Look at me," Cruz says. "You need to trust that I'm going to make sure Joy and Alex get the care required. A Master respects his slave; therefore, I respect your children. Let's try this again differently." He strokes my breasts again. "How does it feel?"

"Good, Master," I say.

"Is that all?" he asks, his eyes disappointed. "Spread your legs."

A fluttering in my stomach. "You could have any woman in the house. What do you want with me?"

"The contract explained," he huffs. "And I told you how to properly ask questions."

"I thought I'd be polishing your boots and cleaning up mostly," I say, staring at the floor.

"There's the problem. Stop thinking and do what I ask. The contract spells out your other duties, and you read it." Cruz's hand and eyes land on my pussy.

"P-p-please don't," I say. Our eyes connect.

A look of concern crosses Cruz's face. "I'm sorry. I should have asked for your consent. I won't do anything you don't want me to do, but I want to touch you. You can tell me to stop if you don't like it, and I promise I will." Cruz never lied to me or anyone else in the house in the eleven months I'd lived there before. He pauses for a few more seconds and makes eye contact. "Do you consent to me touching you, Seven?"

What am I afraid of? I like Cruz. I'd always imagined what it might be like to be with him. I signed a contract. Where's the harm in touching? "Yes, Master." I widen my legs, giving him access. His long fingers walk towards my pussy as my stomach ties itself in knots and my heart beats out of my chest. His fingers skim my fleshy parts. I didn't ask him to stop, and warmth and longing spread throughout me.

"You feel lovely, River, and your sweet scent is divine." He strokes my pussy, chuckling. "Even your pussy hair is white." His observations make me blush. His eyes come back to my face. "You aren't used to discussing such things, are you?"

"Who would I confer with on pussy hair?" I ask.

"No or yes, Master is how you answer," Cruz says. "Husbands, boyfriends, girlfriends, me?" Smiling as he continues touching me.

"We never discussed pussy hair the last time I was here, and I didn't have friends, because my husband never allowed me to. I never left the house, except to jog," I say.

"You're correct. Pussy hair was never a topic of conversation before. Luckily, you have the other girls to be friends with here. Have you ever had an orgasm?" he asks, stroking me.

"I'm forty-four years old, of course I have. I told you yesterday."

"Oh, yes, forgive me for forgetting. Two, you said." He laughs quietly. "Who gave them to you? One of your husbands?"

"Me. I gave them to myself."

"Very nice of you. How, with a vibrator?"

"With my hand," I say. "A little like you're doing."

"Like you were doing last night?" Cruz asks. "Before I made you stop?" My face heats with embarrassment. "Show me," he says, moving his hand away.

"No, ahh, I can't, not in front of you. It's embarrassing."

"You're my slave, which means there's no division between you and me. You'll do what I tell you to do. Now, pleasure yourself." What could I do? I had to follow through, and what did it matter, anyway? I'd taken my clothes off, sat on his lap, let him touch me, and watched him fuck another woman in the ass. Nothing matters anymore. I belong to him. I signed a piece of paper saying so. I probably won't have an orgasm with him watching, anyway.

I bring my hand to my pussy, separate the folds, and locate my clit. Startled by how wet I am, I jerk my head back. He reads my surprise and guesses why. "Nice and wet, I imagine." My cheeks heat more. At home, I had to use massage oil to make myself slick enough, but from simply sitting on Cruz's lap and him stroking me, I'm soaked. I move my index finger across the length of my clit and imagine Cruz's. He whispers in my ear. "I'd like to help some more. May I?"

"I don't know," I say, closing my eyes, trying to block him out. I don't want sex with Cruz. I'm not ready for that intimacy; if he touches me more, he may expect even more.

"Let me finger you. Nothing more, I promise."

Is he reading my mind? Cruz moves his hand towards my pussy, and I can't lie; by this time, my body needs him. After watching him fuck Melanie's ass last night and sitting on his lap, touching me, my body's on fire. Maybe he'd tip the scales and send me over the edge. If he did, I could move off his lap. Problem solved. "Yes," I say.

Cruz's eyes seem to glow, and he grins. He takes his index finger, the one with the skull and butterfly ring, and draws it across my clit, moistening his finger with my juices, and then drifts in. He shoves it in farther and draws it out, in and out, repeating the move over and over, making me want more. "Let's work together on this. I'll follow your tempo," he says, going deeper with every thrust until the coldness and texture of his skull ring hits the entry of my pussy. I keep him inside and clutch his finger with all my might. He chuckles and whispers in my ear, "River wants a second," sending chills up my neck.

"Cruz," I call, working my hips to hold his finger. I groan, but the sound isn't mine. Some other being.

"We're in agreement, but address me as Master." Cruz removes his finger and adds another finger to his first before going back in. There's another ring on this finger, too, a gold metal one, circled with a black nail. He plunges them back into my pussy and brings them out. I press my back against his chest as he drives them in, and my body squeezes to hold them when he takes them away. His touch is exquisite, but I want to get away. Cruz brings his other hand around my waist again, holding me in place, as he draws his fingers in and out of me, and I work my clit frantically with my fingers.

"Oh, please," I groan.

"Please, Master is the correct thing to say," he says. Cruz's lips come to my ear. "Should I let you come, Seven?"

"Please, please, help me, I need to—"

"You do, I agree. Say the proper words."

"Please, Master—"

"I give you permission," he whispers, "but when you climax, keep a clear thought, manifest an intention. It'll assist you in reaching your goals."

"Clear thought?" I ask, frantically rubbing myself. "I think I want to cum."

He growls, "Of course you do, and you shall, but use your sexual energy to do more."

I do what he says, but I don't say it aloud. *I will stand up for myself*, I chant silently in my head.

"I demand you to...to orgasm now!" Cruz yells, forcing his fingers in as deep as he can, spreading them wide inside me, filling my cunt with fingers and rings. A powerful wave sweeps through me like nothing I've experienced before. My pussy pulsates, causing me to rock, almost falling off his lap. I'd have fallen to the floor if he hadn't held me there. Finally, the waves of pleasure stop. I turn my head to meet his. Our foreheads press against one another, our hair undone, strands intertwined.

At first, I'm embarrassed to move, but then I remember I can't go, not until Cruz releases me. He brings his fingers out and holds them up, coated with me, and licks them and his rings. "Your fluids contain magical energy, and yours are the sweetest I've ever tasted. Like honey, but sweeter than any bees." It's a wicked thing and a sweet thing to say. No one has ever said anything like that to me before, making my body tingle and a smile spread within me.

9

CHILDREN OF THE PALACE

CRUZ

"Look, Mr. Cruz, I drew you another picture, look. He's like you. He's a sorcerer. He can do magic."

"Thank you, Joy. Nice. What makes you think I can do magic?"

"My mom said you have special powers."

"She did, did she?"

"Can we have strawberry ice cream? It's my favorite."

"I'll buy some."

"Can I have a unicorn?"

"I'll see what I can do."

"You can do it, I know you can. Can my brother and I play in here? Can we go to the pretend jail?"

"Glad you like it, but that's a crate for my dog. I'll take you two for an outing. We can walk to the zoo from here, you know." *Fuck.* Chains on walls are not suitable for children. The crate needs to go, too. And where the hell will I get a unicorn?

"Is the dog outside?" Alex asks.

"What's his name?" Joy asks. "Did you make him disappear?"

"It's not here at the moment. Sorry, but I've got work to do now. Could you play in your room? Thank you."

I shut the door and lock it. Shit. Having children in the house is more of a problem than expected. What if they had come in when I had River in a compromising position? I need to remember to keep the door locked when she's with me.

What I did with River has left me perplexed. My pleasuring a woman only happens when she's in my family of sex workers, and I'm trying to cheer her up or coerce her into doing something she doesn't want to do. River's my slave and should please me. Instead, she refused to tell me how she got the marks. I should have punished her immediately for that. A slave answers all questions her Master poses. What the fuck is wrong with me? A woman in my house earns her orgasm, and River hasn't. My plan to edge her and put her on the ropes for a while backfired. I wanted to draw it out and make her needy, but my need put that idea to bed. The other problem, I enjoyed every minute of getting River off. She shot all over my leg. Difficulty climaxing? Ha. If she does, it's her asshole husband's fault. She had no problem with me, and it had nothing to do with magic. I smile.

I loved making her undress in front of me, too. Unfortunately, when she's perfect, I won't be interested anymore. She got all embarrassed, squirmed on my lap, and jumped off. She told me precisely what bothered her most, another wrong move, and I thought she was more thoughtful. Since humiliation is her bug-a-boo, I'll do it again to gain control and punish her.

The sooner I stick my cock in River, the better. The last woman who had control of me was Gloria, who gave me everything, taught me the business, then tried to take it away. I'm spending too much time thinking about River. That can't be a good thing.

"River, I've sent you three messages to come to my room. Why didn't you?"

"I'm sorry, I had to attend to Alex and Joy. Help them with their workbooks. I homeschool, and I can't find my phone and—"

"I don't want excuses. 'I'm sorry, Master' is all I want to hear. You make yourself available to me at all times, day or night. Just because you sat on my lap and I stuck my finger in your cunt means nothing. I've done the same to thousands of others, and there's nothing special about yours." River's shoulders slump, and her face drops and turns red. Too easy to bring her to her knees. Where's the fun? And since it's not, I need to stop. Remember, "don't be mean." *I need realistic expectations. She's a mother. Her children must come first.*

"I told you, my phone's missing. I had it last night, but now I can't find it. You don't have to be crude," River says.

"Slaves don't talk back. Don't correct your Master, ever." This time, she lowers her eyes. Maybe she did lose her phone. "What's your number?" She gives it to me, and I say, "Go next door and listen for the ring."

I hold the phone to my ear, and a minute later, she returns. "It's not there," she says. "I don't understand it. It was on the floor when I fell asleep."

I go to my desk drawer, pull out a new burner phone, key the burner phone's numbers into mine, forward the texts, and toss the new cell to her. "Problem solved. Read the texts I sent you immediately. Those are your slave tasks today. Get busy."

I turn my back on her and walk to the shower. I have a meeting. Some heavy hitters want a partner to open a sex shop/dungeon in River North. I can make a lot of money, not that I need any more, but the Italian boys want the deal, and I need to keep them happy. I might require their muscle in the future.

When I leave the shower, my balls are tight. After assisting River in orgasming earlier, I need one of my own. I pick up my phone to call a woman, but I remember I don't need to. River's sitting in the other room. I wrap my towel around my bottom half, stride to my throne, and sit. She's on the floor, rubbing polish over one of my boots. A piece of her hair falls in front of her face. She tilts her head up, and her blue eyes meet mine. For a brief instant, I read fear, which ignites my fervor further.

"Seven, come here," I say, pointing in front of me. I see River hesitate, and because she does, I change my instructions. "Crawl."

"What?"

"You heard me. Stay on your knees, get on your hands and crawl." Her eyes get angry, and I ignore them. "Kneel right here." I point at the floor in front of me. Her head is in the perfect position for what I want her for. Her eyes waver and then close and open as she looks up. "I'm sure you've done this before," taking the towel off.

Her face grows even redder as she views my cock and realizes what she's here to do. "Not completely," she says.

"What the hell does that mean?" I ask, attempting to control my laughter.

"I mean, I tried with my date after prom in high school, but my mother saw and stopped—"

"I get the picture."

"The other times, my first husband was too sick and he couldn't...and my second husband didn't want—"

"Enough of the history, Seven. Suffice to say, this time you'll complete the job. How does my cock compare to your prom date and your husband's, since you feel compelled to stare at it instead of at the floor?" I ask, smirking.

"Mmm, I'm not sure. Possibly smaller than my dates, but the car was dark, and he was on the football team." Her eyes waver. "And my first husband was ill, like I said. Because of his pain, we smoked pot, and maybe that made it look bigger."

"How about husband number two?" I laugh. No way these dudes had larger cocks than mine. River is playing with me. I can play, too.

"He's tiny," she answers, looking directly at my cock. "And he only wanted me to squeeze his—"

"Enough. Eyes down." I know what River is doing, trying to make me lose my erection. "Seven, give me your hand." She makes a weird expression and pauses. "What's the problem? You wanted to touch me before without asking. Now I want you to touch me, and you don't want to?"

"I'm nervous," she says.

"I'll help you. If you follow instructions, this will be over quickly. Give me your hand." Her hand comes up slowly. I place her hand in mine, and her pulse races. I bring our hands to my cock and together stroke the length of it. "See, just like you did before." I let go of her hand. After she brings her hand up and down on my shaft several times, I provide more instruction. "Squeeze harder and focus on the head. Good girl. See the pre-cum? Rub it into your palm. Good. Your hand will move more smoothly now, and my enjoyment will increase. Now caress my balls. Very good. You're doing great. As much as I love your hand, I want your lips. Do you want to suck on me, Seven?"

Her eyebrows shoot upward. "Can't I just use my hand?" Her eyes waver.

"You're my slave. You do what I request, and I've expressed what I wish. Do you consent or not?"

"How?" she asks.

"Glad you asked. Pretend you're licking an ice cream cone." Her face turns redder as she brings her lips closer, peering at me through her blonde lashes. Her tongue comes out of her mouth hesitantly, and from there she licks the length of my cock. Her touch and her eyes undo me, and truthfully, I could cum right now if I wanted to. The intensity of her expression and the softness of her slippery, apple-red tongue...But I stop myself.

"Very good. Now you're going to suck on the head. Take your mouth, swirl your tongue around it, and then suck. Vary things, that's good." If River was telling the truth that she hasn't done this much, she's a natural.

"I want you to suck on my balls now. First, lick them one at a time, then suck them." River's touch is gentle, and after a minute, I challenge her. "Now suck on both balls simultaneously but go slow and be gentle...it's a very sensitive part of a man's anatomy." Somehow, she gets them both in her mouth, but she can barely move her tongue, and her teeth scrape them. After a minute, I let her be, touching her shoulder and pulling away, my swollen balls dropping back out of her mouth one at a time.

"Now, this part is trickier. I want you to slide my entire cock into your mouth. You'll have to scoot up and position yourself over me to bring my cock down your throat. Oh, good start." She's only gotten halfway, but she's a rookie, and I'm on the larger size, no matter what she says. "Now go deeper, but you don't want to gag. I know this is your first time with me. Do the best you can. Take me in your throat." River drops her entire mouth over my swollen dick, taking me in farther this time. I touch the back of her head and guide her. "I'm not going to force you, but I'm going to show you. Changing the rhythm, understand?" I guide her head into moving faster, slower, then farther, until she has the idea. I can feel my cock growing even harder. "Can you go further? Thatta girl."

A few more strokes and River will have me. "Seven, I'm going to come. Swallow my cum if you can. It's going to taste salty. If you don't want to, use the towel to contain it." I let myself go. She grasps my cock with one hand. As it contracts, she gulps every bit of cum streaming out, not allowing a drop or spill. Her performance surprises and impresses me. I've trained many girls in the art of fellatio. They all started with more experience, but River is different...special. Is it her warm mouth, soft lips, innocence, or ability to follow my instructions perfectly?

Suddenly, she pulls away, and I say, "Don't move. Remember, you don't go until I say you can." She needs to learn that she isn't in control of her own movements. Minutes pass, and I keep her in front of me on her knees while I scroll through my text messages.

"May I please use the bathroom?" River asks.

"Almost correct. Try again."

"Master, may I please use the bathroom?"

"Not yet." At the fifteen-minute mark, I finally let River go, and she runs towards the bathroom and shuts the door while I move to my desk. When she returns, I smell a hint of toothpaste. "Next time, ask me if you can brush your teeth after you give me a blowjob. I might want to taste myself. Our fluids are special, not to be wasted. Also, no closing doors. You don't need privacy; you're my slave and belong to me." Her gaze flits around the room. "Answer me."

"Yes, Master," she responds, her eyes downwards.

I may have pushed her away with my actions, but making subs and slaves wait and tearing away their defenses is how you gain control over them, heighten their sexual response, and put them in a meditative state. "Come here."

River walks towards me, and I notice her eyes. A faraway look again. Was I pushing too hard and moving too fast again? She needs my praise and solace. "You did well, River. Go inside the circle, to the altar, and say a prayer for me, yourself, and everyone in the house. Light a candle and smudge the room with sage when you're done, to remove any negative energy."

I watch as she kneels before my altar, lights the Goddess and

God candles, bows before the plant and antlers positioned in the center, and touches the athame, my black ceremonial blade, in the top left to garner strength. She closes her eyes and goes within. A few minutes later, she walks the smoking sage through the room, spending more minutes by my chair where she'd pleasured herself and me. When she's done, she places the sage in the bowl on the altar.

She goes to the window and looks out, but her eyes are still distant. I grab her arm, push her towards the bed, and fall on top. She panics and struggles against me, lashing out, trying to grapple with me. She strikes me in my chest with her hands and tries to kick me with her feet, bringing forth another memory of when I fought Gloria and pinned her to the wall.

"You promised!" River screams. "You said you wouldn't hurt me!" She tosses herself back and forth.

Finally, I've had enough. I capture her hands and hold them against the mattress. She tries to knee me, and I place my legs on her. She's defenseless. Her face crumples, and tears spill when she realizes it. I know I've frightened her, and I regret it immediately.

"I'm sorry," I say. "I don't want to hurt you. I need you close after what we shared." She stops struggling. I let go of her hands, and she rolls to my side and lays her head on the pillow. I pull her closer, and she brings her head to my chest. A few minutes later, I whisper River's name. No response. She's fallen asleep. I don't wake her. She needs her rest.

When she wakes an hour later, I text Bones to delay the meeting. I'll be late. Before I leave, I prepare a calming charm with chamomile, lavender, peppermint, and rose quartz. I hand River the tiny glass bottle and fold her fingers around it. "Keep this on you," I say. "It'll help." I bring her close, and she accepts my embrace.

As Tito drives me to the meeting later, I glance out the window and see all the ordinary people, the ones with wives, regular jobs, and children. River has pushed me off my game. I'm not treating her like all the others. My other women all have pretty faces and warm holes that will eventually support the house and become a part of my family, or if they remain slaves, sold to others. I should've realized neither of those scenarios is possible with River. The problem, the one I don't want to admit, I want River with me, and wanting to fuck her isn't the only reason. I never know what to expect from her. She's called me on some of my bullshit in the past, but she never deliberately meant to. As I said, she's submissive. What will happen if she impedes my business? Am I weak? You can trust only one person in this world: yourself.

I try to forget River. The fact that I can't angers me. Will she attempt to destroy me as Gloria had?

IO
CHARMED LIFE

RIVER

I've finished polishing all of Cruz's boots. I swear, he's the male Imelda Marcos of Chicago. Should I tell him that? He probably won't think it's funny. He's earnest and seems to do everything he can not to laugh. Truthfully, I probably shouldn't be laughing either, but remembering how he touched me and I touched him makes me giddy. I'm ridiculous. Cruz can't care about someone like me. On my first day as a slave, I let him touch me; on day two, I gave him a blowjob. What will I do on day three? How does he do it? How does he control me like that? What a stupid question. Nothing and nobody seems to scare him; that's how he does it. Maybe he is a witch, like he says.

I go to his bookshelf and find his book of spells. The last time I was here, I used the love spell on him, but I must have done something wrong; it worked in reverse, affected me instead. I go to his candle drawer and find the one I'm looking for, a pink one. On his desk, I find notepaper and a pencil and write both of our names on it, Cruz MacKenzie and River Rogers, drawing a circle around it. I light the small pink candle and place it on the altar. I close my eyes and envision Cruz and me together as I clutch the paper.

This time, I imagine it better because we've been together. I think of Cruz's eyes gleaming when he watched me, his fingers burning as they explored my body, and later, my mouth on his cock as I licked his shaft, feeling like electricity. I shift my attention to afterward, him letting me know he needs me, bringing me into his arms as we lay on the bed, the way our hearts beat as one as I fell asleep on his chest. I repeat the chant: *Our fate is sealed. We are one. It must be true. It is done.*

The candle slowly burns down and goes out. I lick my fingers and press the wick to make sure, then straighten up the altar area.

I remind myself that getting close to Cruz is a gamble. From living with him before, I know he's the most successful person in the sex trade in Chicago or the entire Midwest. If it involves sex and women, he's involved. I take the charm he made and study the tiny bottle. He says it will help me. Hopefully by the end of all this, I won't have traded one devil for another one. Can anyone or anything keep my anxiety in check? Another world is contained inside the glass. I let myself go, imagining myself living inside of—

Knock knock. I hurriedly stuffed the charm deep in my pocket.

"Hey, you didn't come to dinner," Gia says, coming through the door and staring at the floor. "Wow, you polished all these? There's gotta be fifty pairs of shoes and boots here."

"Actually, there's fifty-five, but who's counting?" I laugh. "What time is it?"

"Eight-thirty," Gia says.

"Oh, my God. I forgot to give dinner to Alex and Joy." I start running towards the door.

"Don't worry," Gia says, taking my hand and pulling me toward the center of the room. "They ate with us at five. Lydia let them watch TV for a while, then read them a story, and they're in their room now, getting ready for bed. If you want to check on them later. We assumed you were on lockdown."

"I don't understand what happened." I give a loud sigh. "I'm a negligent mother to forget my own children."

"Taking a break from your kids for a couple of hours while other people are watching them is not negligence, River. Besides, it's not your fault. You lose your perspective when you..." She puts an arm around me. "But I'm not supposed to talk about that. Cruz wants me to monitor you, so here I am."

"Talk about what?"

Gia looks towards the wall where the chains and the cage in the room's corner are located. "When you didn't show up for dinner, I thought maybe you were..." She pauses. "I gotta go," she finishes, opening the door and slipping out.

I check the burner phone Cruz gave me to review the task list. I've only completed one of the five tasks. The next one is to organize the closet. First, I return all the shoes and boots to their shelves, then I examine the rest of the space. It needs organization. Some of the drawers are open, and I can see various items mixed together and clothes sloppily hanging halfway out of them. It's a big job, so I decide to wait and check on the children first.

Alex and Joy are finished with all the assignments in their workbooks. They tell me they went on a walk to the park and then to the grocery store with Gia. Joy excitedly recounts seeing an old woman walking her cat on a leash on the sidewalk. They show me the books Cruz let them borrow from his library on dinosaurs and Japan. I haven't seen either of them this happy in a long time, and it makes me believe I've done the right thing, coming here.

I return to Cruz's room an hour later, after tucking the children in. I'm not ready to sleep. I go to his closet and remove all the items from their drawers. I make a pile out of clothing too worn to keep. I then put all the remaining T-shirts in one place, underwear in another, socks in another, and so on. By the time I finish, and everything's folded and placed back in their correct drawers, I check the time; one in the morning, and Cruz still isn't home.

I go to the bathroom, wash my face, brush my teeth, and come back, and I notice the mat by the bed with the small pillow. I'd sleep there, not in Cruz's bed, unless he invites me. I'm still deciding which I'd prefer. I turn the light off and lie down on the mat.

"River, River," someone whispers, the perfume from before in the air again. I must have drifted off. I hear a tapping sound, like metal on glass.

"What?" I call out. I look towards the windows, and it's still black outside. I don't have my watch anymore, so I reach for my phone but can't locate it. Footsteps come down the hall, drawing nearer and getting louder. The door opens, but no one is there, and the doorway remains empty. The overwhelming scent of thousands of roses hit my nose again. The room suddenly grows colder, and two windows in the bathroom open, then bang shut. My head is killing me. The door slams closed. I climb from the floor and creep towards the bathroom window. No one is there. Maybe the drafty windows blew the door open. But when I check the windows, I see they're locked, covered with condensation. How did they blow open? I'm cold and my head throbs.

I searched the cabinet for aspirin, lit by the nightlight. Nothing. I catch my image in the mirror and stagger back, shocked. My reflection is all wrong. Half my face is me, and the other half is someone else, the red-haired woman. But she's pale, her flesh is rotting, her eyes are bulging, and blood is running from her nose. "Don't trust him," she says.

I sprint from the bathroom and pace, questioning my hallucination. Am I not awake? Is it a migraine headache? I talk myself into returning to the bathroom to check again and snap on the light switch. I touch the mirror when I see myself whole, relieved to see only me and hear nothing but my own heartbeat. I turn the light off and leave the bathroom. I know I can't go back to sleep. My head is spinning. I have three items remaining on my task list. Should I complete them? The next task is to clean the bathroom. I shudder as I head back in.

CRUZ

The Italians know how to party, especially Angelo. You can't say no when they want to celebrate and bring out their best whores for you. This one had giant tits, but the whole time I had her bent over the table, balls deep, my only wish was that I was home with River. It's now close to five a.m., and my chest burns the whole way back in the car to The Palace. Heartburn? I'd made the mistake of mentioning I had a new slave to Angelo, and now he's pressing me to let him have a turn.

Bones and Gia are standing in the kitchen when I arrive, which isn't unusual. Both are early risers. Gia enjoys yoga every morning, and Bones likes to roam the house, snooping.

"How did it go with Angelo?" Bones asks.

"We have a deal. What's going on here? How were earnings last night?"

Besides not answering, I notice Bones and Gia exchanging looks with one another. "Ahhh, there might be a problem with River," Gia says, "but I can't say for sure."

"What problem?" I ask, a knot in my belly.

"She missed dinner last night, and when I went to her room later that evening, she didn't know what time it was. She'd polished fifty-five pairs of your shoes. And she was still up at two-thirty this morning cleaning your room, and when I checked a few minutes ago, she was still awake. I don't think she slept at all, and she didn't eat dinner or breakfast, either. At this rate, she's going to go down fast if…"

"Are you telling me how to break a slave and be a Master, Gia?" I ask, my heart beating faster.

Gia's head turns away. "I wouldn't dare, but we both know she's fragile, and you asked me to monitor her. If she doesn't take care of herself, she could—"

"She's my slave, not yours. The first week of training is challenging. Breaking a person and building them into something better is difficult. I'll take your concerns under advisement. Fix coffee, tea, and breakfast for two and bring the tray to my room. Thank you." I walk away, knowing I've acted unfairly aggressively towards Gia to mask my self-loathing. I failed to care for my slave correctly.

II

JOPHIEL

CRUZ

I see her. River's standing on a chair, her arm stretched out, head tilted up towards the chandelier, like Jophiel, archangel of creativity, beauty, and art, showing me the way.

"Seven, get down from there." As I call, she loses her balance and falls, the chair tilting too. I run towards her and scoop her up before she hits the floor. Holding her in my arms, her body relaxes into mine, and she wraps her arms around my neck.

I examine her face, it's drawn and pale, and I look away from her and replay my conversation with Angelo, wishing I could go back and undo it.

"I'm sorry, Master, for not kneeling," her face now worried. 'I didn't see you."

"What were you doing?"

"Cleaning the glass on the chandelier. I noticed it was dusty. I finished everything else."

"Did you sleep?" I ask as I carry and place her on the bed.

"A little, but I heard something and woke up. Once I did, I couldn't go to sleep again. I didn't want to disappoint you by not completing everything."

"Well done for staying with it," I say. I push down the urge to correct River for not sleeping and eating. Did I make the wrong charm? I thought I chose one to banish anxiety, not to increase energy or make her more compliant.

Knock knock.

Gia delivers the tray, the whole time staring at me. "Place it on the table, thank you," I say to her.

After she leaves, I turn and face River. "First, we're going to have breakfast, then a bath, and then sleep." I sit on the throne and point to my lap. River approaches me hesitantly and sits on my knees. I see her eyes waver back and forth with anxiety. I hand her an egg sandwich on an English muffin, and she seems relieved I'm not feeding it to her. Or is it something else?

"I saw something last night." She pauses. "It was disturbing."

"My porno collection?" I ask, trying to crack a joke and give myself time to imagine what could have frightened her.

She gets a funny expression on her face, blinking, and her mouth opens. "No. The mirror in your bathroom. Is it a trick one, the kind they have in funhouses that can distort your face?"

"Of course not. Why do you ask?"

"I...saw something after I woke up to get an aspirin and water. It was me, but it wasn't. Only half my face was me, and the other part was another woman, but deformed."

"Maybe you weren't fully awake yet." I didn't mention my other thought, that becoming my slave is causing the kind of stress to make her personality split. I pour her some green tea, which seems to be her preference, and pass her the cup. "The room looks lovely, better than ever," I say, changing the subject.

"Thank you. I tried to put your items where you would. I hope I did it right."

"I'm sure you did." She seems eager to change the subject, too. The room doesn't smell or look the same. River's presence, like perfume, permeates the space. Everything is clean, dusted, and in its proper place. A sense of well-being crept inside of me after tasting failure earlier. How did River know their proper places? Somehow, she did. Even the windows sparkle. Usually, I keep the shades drawn. Today they're open, and the sun shines in, making everything lighter. But that's not who I am.

"Should I run the bathwater, Master?"

Flabbergasted. I didn't expect River to transform this quickly. "No, you wait here and rest." I walk to the bathroom. It's like my bedroom—spotless. The tile sparkles, and the grout's white. The towels are rolled and placed in a basket, as they show in some of those home-decorator magazines. She knows how to do shit and get things done better than any of the other slaves I've had before. Maybe because she's older than the others.

I run the water, throw in a bath bomb for us to enjoy, and turn on the jets. I check the back of my door. I only have one robe. I proceed to my closet. Shit, my closet has never been this organized. I open the drawers, and see everything I own folded perfectly; my Ts, my jockeys, everything. I select one of my dress shirts from a hanger and bring it to the bathroom for her to slip into after our bath. I return to the bedroom, to the small refrigerator, remove two bottles of spring water, and take her hand. Gia is right; I need to rein River in before she self-destructs. The hallucinations are an alarming sign of stress.

I undress, and River stands, watching the water fill the tub. "Remove your clothing, Seven. Climb in and relax."

"Maybe I can take one after you, Master."

"Is that what you want?" I ask.

"I don't know…uhm, I'm not sure," she says, stumbling over her words.

As Master, I know I should tell my slave to get in the damn

bathtub, but now isn't the time to lower the boom. I climb into the tub, turn off the water, and settle in. A couple of minutes pass, and finally River peels her clothing off with her back turned away from me. I see the scars again. Anger fills me. *Did her husband give her those?* She turns around, walks towards the tub, steps in, and lowers herself into the water, the bubbles surrounding her.

"How does it feel?" I ask.

"Wonderful."

I open and pass her the bottled water, "Drink this, River. Let's check in with each other. This is your 'free period.' You can say whatever you need to say without concerning yourself with retribution." She takes a sip and holds the bottle, but says nothing. "I'm thrilled with your initiative. No slave I've ever had has ever worked as hard to please me, especially so quickly. You've done an amazing job, but—"

"I knew there was a 'but' coming," she says, lowering her head and dropping her shoulders.

"Are you interrupting me?" I ask, and she shakes her head no. "When I list tasks for you to do, unless I set a time limit, you do them at your own leisure. You'll eat all meals, breakfast, lunch, and dinner, and go to sleep by ten. Understand?"

"Yes. I've failed." Her lips tighten into a grimace. "Are you displeased?"

"No, *I* failed *you*. As your Master, I should've made my expectations and instructions clear. I apologize, and I hope you'll forgive me. Do you?"

Her head rises, and she looks at me with moist eyes. "Yes, if you forgive me the next time I do something wrong."

"You mean a kind of 'get out of jail free' card?" I ask, our eyes meeting.

"Yes."

"Deal. Do you have anything else you need to say? Questions, concerns about anything?"

"No."

"Free time is over, then." I pick up the soap, running the bar along her arm until she pulls away. "Stay still," I say.

"I can wash myself."

"I want to clean you."

"Please, Cruz—"

"It's Master again now. You can clean me after I'm done with you," I say, and she seems calmer. "Lift your arms." As she does, I rub soap under them, then rinse them off with a cloth. I go under her breasts and the front of her torso. I bring the soap inside her legs. "Spread wider." When she does, I rub it on her pussy, then rinse her and place the soap on the edge of the tub. I take her hand, holding it. "I have an important dinner this weekend with business clients, and I want you at my side."

"Me?" Her eyes register surprise.

"Yes, and you'll need to dress for the occasion, something special, so we need to go out and find something." When Angelo and the Italians see River, they'll see first-hand why my houses outperform theirs. Still, the other reason she has to attend... I screwed up.

I pass her the soap. "My turn now," she says.
***

After I wrap her in a towel, dry her off, and help her on with my shirt, I walk her to my bed and pull back the covers. "Get in."

"Please, let me sleep over here," she says, walking and pointing at the mat.

I bring her back, wrap my arms around her, and pat her back, attempting to soothe her. "We'll use the bed for sleep. We've both been up all night," I say, guessing her concerns. River's eyes brighten, and she relaxes her shoulders. She climbs in, and I cover her. I pull the shades down and climb in next to her, pressing in close while spooning, my cock against her ass. At first, she stiffens; after several minutes, her body softens, collapses into me, and in no time at all she's out.

I leave the bed, pour myself some rum, sit on the edge of the mattress, study her face, and connect the three freckles on her nose, making an imaginary triangle. My cock throbs. I pinch a piece of her hair between my index and forefinger and study the strands. The same color as mine, but more flexible. I hope her willingness to explore sexual acts is the same. In my world, all acts of love are acceptable because of the great goddess, but I'm fearful River thinks differently.

I need to get clearer about my directions to River and my intentions. After my experience with my mother and Gloria, people's suffering made me feel good and took away some of my hurt. As I got older, though, I learned to control my demons. I learned that to get people to follow my orders, I had to earn their respect. To do that, I couldn't hurt them. I treat members of my household better than my family or Gloria ever treated theirs. Still, sometimes the devil comes to play, and someone's suffering becomes my entertainment. Do I want River to suffer? Or do I want to give her pleasure? What do I want River for? Is she here solely for amusement?

12
VIRGIN & ENEMIES

"Mommy, Mommy. Wake up. Look what Mr. Cruz bought me. A unicorn balloon. Isn't it pretty, Mommy? Look."

I open one eye. The giant silver and pink metallic unicorn balloon floats from a long pink ribbon above Joy's head. "Beautiful. Where did you get it?"

"Mr. Cruz bought us each something special when he took us out for dinner. Isn't it cool?"

"When?"

"Last night."

"What time is it?"

She adorably shrugs. "I not know."

"You mean you don't know."

"I don't know!"

"You're up, I see." Cruz comes into the room with Alex, carrying a tray. "Are you hungry? I have some oatmeal and tea. You've been asleep since yesterday."

I panic. I search Cruz's eyes for anger, but there's none. "I'm so sorry. Thanks for taking the children out to dinner last night. It was sweet of you."

Cruz comes close, hands me the cup of tea, and lowers his voice. "You know, sweetness has nothing to do with my actions. One does what one has to do to maintain order and harmony in one's house. I told you before, I take my responsibility as your Master seriously, and the care of your children, too." He turns to Alex and Joy. "Kids, take your new toys to your room while Seven prepares herself to meet the day."

"Her name's not Seven!" my daughter says, rolling her eyes. "It's Mommy!"

"Of course it is. Seven's a nickname, love," Cruz says.

I wrap the sheet tighter around my body. "Do as Mr. Cruz says."

After they leave, Cruz asks, "What's Joy's fascination with unicorns?"

"I guess she's seduced by their magical properties."

"It seems her mother's into magical properties, too."

"What do you mean?" Does Cruz suspect I cast a love spell the other day?

"Joy mentioned that you said I was a sorcerer and had magical powers."

"You practice Wicca. I was just putting it into a language my daughter could understand." I blush.

"I thought you might be referring to something else. I did some research, and interestingly, the unicorn symbolizes joy, her name. Crazy the way she's drawn to them." Cruz chuckles. "If they were real, she'd be the only one in The Palace who could capture one."

"True. Only a virgin can approach a unicorn," I smile. "She likes rainbows too; did you buy one of those?" I pretend to look out the window. "What was your favorite toy when you were a child?" I ask.

Cruz's top lip curls. He swallows hard, his eyes deaden. "Anything taking my eyes off of God, my father banned from the house." As quickly as the anger comes, his scowl disappears, and his tone becomes friendly again. "Get up. We need to find you a dress, shoes, and accessories." Then he seems to catch himself. "And, so you don't become confused in the future, from now on, I expect you to rise before me in the morning, at seven-thirty a.m., and bring me coffee. Therefore, like I said yesterday, you will not skip sleep in the future, which caused this scenario again. You've now used your 'get out of jail for free' card. Are we clear?"

"Yes, Master."

"Where are we going?" I ask half an hour later as I sit in the back of a large cherry cola-colored Suburban with Cruz while one of his crew drives and another sits in the passenger's seat.

"It's 'where are we going, Master?' Are you forgetting on purpose? The side streets of the Magnificent Mile have several boutiques where we can find something appropriate," he says, glancing out the window.

"I apologize, Master. I sew well. I could have borrowed something from one of the other girls and done alterations."

"I'm sure you do, but this is a special dinner, and you must look your best. Not that you wouldn't look good in a paper bag."

"Sometimes, Cruz, you can say the sweetest things, and then other times..." I look out the window. "I'm sorry, what I meant to say is Master."

"Be careful, slave. You don't want to ruin the day." He grabs my hand, pulls me towards him, and nuzzles my ear.

Everything I try on at the boutiques where Cruz takes me makes me look fat, or worse yet, like I'm trying to be someone I'm not, until the last one. He selects a dress there that's light, pale pink, and gauzy. I look like me, but a better version, if that makes any sense. "You look like a princess," he says.

The organza floats around my body. I glance at the price tag. "Oh ho ho, I don't think so," I say while laughing, shaking my head.

"Why not? It's perfect," he frowns.

"The price is ridiculous. How many men will the women in the house have to fuck to pay for this dress?"

Cruz's nostrils flare, and his eyes narrow. "I decide what to purchase, not you, Seven. You wear the dress I buy." He hands the dress and his credit card to the saleswoman and shoots me a warning look.

He buys me silver sandals at another store, and I know better than to say anything about their cost. "I have jewelry at the house you can select from," he says as we return to the car with the shoes.

"Thank you for the dress. It's beautiful, Master."

"I'm sure your husbands bought you nice attire."

"My first one died too soon, and we spent all our money trying to cure him. The second one made me buy my clothes at thrift shops. Once or twice, I found something nice."

"He's a wealthy man." Cruz rubs his chin and scratches his temple. "He could afford to spend thousands on a dress."

"He could, but he didn't. He didn't want me to look attractive. 'I don't want other men looking at you,' he said more than once. Last year, he changed to a different tactic. 'You're old and fat. New clothes won't improve anything.' He was right."

"Sounds like a charmer. Obviously, he's an idiot." Cruz shakes his head back and forth. "I think I mentioned before that I don't want you speaking badly about yourself. I don't like it." Then he changes the subject and holds my hand. "I'm ready for afternoon tea," he chirps.

When we arrive at the Walnut Room at the top of the old Marshall Field building, people are in line to get inside. I notice all the women are wearing better clothes than me. I've got on jeans, an old peacoat, and dirty sneakers. "I'm not dressed for this," I say, motioning to the other people.

"When you're a beautiful woman, you needn't worry about things like that." His comment makes me laugh, but Cruz doesn't laugh back, staring at me with unwavering eye contact. "It's not a joke. If you still have concerns, I'll lend you my suit jacket. It cost five thousand dollars." Cruz takes it off, stands tall with a gleam in his eyes, and wraps the jacket around my shoulders. Some women in line watch him do this and smile at me. His doing that makes me blush and feel worthy.

Once at our table, Cruz orders the high tea buffet for both of us. A tuxedoed waiter comes by with a cart filled with trays—artichoke tarts, quiche, cookies, smoked salmon, and the choices just keep going on and on. "We can sneak some out for your children," he says, smiling.

"Master, what's this business dinner I'm wearing the dress to?"

"I'd rather not talk business right now. What we need to do is discuss your husband. Since you lost your phone, he can't call you, but I've hired an attorney to represent you. At some point, your husband or his friends will learn where you are. I've given the attorney the bare-bones facts, and he's going to see if we can gain temporary custody until the court can investigate. But it could also go the other way, as your husband mentioned. There's a small chance you could get charged with kidnapping. Not likely, because of the bruises on the children, but it could happen. I sent the attorney photos, and with what the children are saying, the attorney believes your case appears strong, but your husband could say we've coached them."

"Yes, Master, he could. The last text I got from Jack, before I lost my cell, said he knew I was in Chicago."

"I'll double up on security," Cruz says. "Next time, tell me these things earlier."

MYSTERY MAN & JACK PEARSON

"Who is this? How did you get my wife's phone?"

"I have her."

"Who are you?"

"I'm not ready to say, but we can make a deal."

"What kind of deal?"

"I'm ready to return your children if you let me keep River and help me get rid of my boss. How does that sound?

"An interesting proposition. My wife would continue to be a problem if she came back, anyway. Who's the man you want to get rid of?"

"Do we have a deal?"

"That depends. Who's the man I have to get rid of?"

"Cruz MacKenzie."

"His name sounds familiar... Oh yes, I remember now. He runs women, yes?"

"That's the one."

"This is fantastic. My wife leaves me and lands in the arms of a pimp."

"Let me make myself clear. If I help you with this, everything MacKenzie owns comes to me, including River."

"I won't get in the way. I'm a businessperson. I simply want my children back."

"Then we have a deal?"

"Yes, definitely. But let me be clear. I don't want my wife back."

"I'll text you again later on this phone."

13
ROUGH

CRUZ

"Place the dress on the bed," I say when we return to The Palace. River removes the gown from the bag and the light pink organza floats, skimming the floor before landing on my burgundy comforter. I go to my safe, bring several boxes out, and place them on the bed next to the dress.

"Pick some jewels to wear with the dress," I say. Gloria invested heavily in gems and jewelry of all sorts. Some pieces are exceedingly gaudy, others beautifully minimalist. It'll be interesting to see what River selects.

"The dress is beautiful by itself, Master. I don't need—"

"I told you what to do. Do it."

She opens the boxes hesitantly, her mouth dropping open as she picks up each dazzling piece, then places them back in their containers and moves on. This continues for a few more minutes until she comes to a large, single baroque black pearl on a silver chain.

"This," she says, holding it in front of the window, swirls of pink and violet bouncing off the gray crevices of the pearl.

"Try it on," I say, placing it around her neck and fastening the clasp.

The pearl drops between her breasts, and River's cheeks turn pink. "I don't know, maybe—"

"Perfect," I say. "Find some earrings, a ring, or a bracelet." I watch as she opens more boxes and puts items aside. I approve of her choices. The earrings are small, light-gray baroque pearls hanging from silver threads. Silver bangle stacked bracelets complete the outfit.

"This is enough," she says, looking at me as if waiting for my opinion.

"I agree. Good choices."

Her face lights up. "Thank you for letting me borrow them." She puts everything else back in the boxes.

"I'm giving them to you. I can't imagine anyone else wearing any of them."

I can't put this off any longer and don't want to. Watching her model the dresses has lit a fire within me. I take my shirt off and remove my favorite flogger from the shelf, the purple deerskin one. The terror on River's face as her eyes drift across the piece unnerves me. I've never seen that expression on any of the others like that, just the opposite, and I flog them often. River runs for the door. "Stop right there," I call. As she does, her back is to me, and her body shakes.

"Please...Master, what did I do wrong?" she asks. "Was it what I said in the car, forgetting to call you Master, not wanting the dress, or did I select the wrong jewelry? What, what did I do?" Her body heaves as she fires her questions.

"Turn around and come stand in front of me. I'm not conversing with your back." Tears are already forming, and she blinks them away. "Kneel. You did nothing wrong. This—" I hold the flogger in both hands under her nose— "has nothing to do with pain or punishment. You'll like the feeling, and eventually even crave the leather's caress. I promise you. Put your hands out." As her fingers spring from her clenched fist, I run the flogger's tails across them. "Feel the softness of the leather. When the flails land on your back, they'll be soft too, like a massage. It'll feel nothing like the crop or the whip. If it's going to hurt, I'd tell you. Now remove your clothes, Seven."

I take the leather handcuffs, the pink ones lined with lambswool, out next and buckle them on her wrists and ankles as her eyes fill with fear. "Please, I promise. I won't run again," she says, her naked skin blossoming in goosebumps.

"I know you won't. Climb on the bed and lie on your stomach." I ignore her begging. After she does it reluctantly, I snap the bed's chains onto the handcuffs, secure her feet as well, and draw them all tighter. Her body trembles.

"Why do you have to chain me down?" River asks.

"Try it. If you don't like it, I'll let you loose." I place my flogger in front of her face. "Smell the leather, River." Then I drag the tresses across her face and bring the shaft to her mouth. "Kiss it for me, River." Her lips quiver before they touch the shaft.

I can't recall wanting to possess anyone as much as I want her right now. The creamy white skin on her magnificent ass still has the bruises I'd given her two days ago, but they've faded to pink. If I flog her correctly, it will leave no marks, only reddening her skin.

I step closer and drag the falls across the scars on her back. She flinches. She'll face her fear. Someone has whipped her before, and not with any flogger or even a crop. Not with love; with hate. I drape the deerskin tails lower on her back, then drag them to her buttocks and calves, and finally the soles of her feet and back, stopping between her thighs. Sighs escape her mouth, and she closes her eyes, relaxing into what I'm doing.

I step further from her. "I'm going to flog you now, but it

shouldn't hurt. If it does, tell me immediately, and use your safe word. Do you consent, Seven?

"Yes, Master."

"What's your safe word?"

"Gothic," River says.

I bring my arm back behind my head, and then forward, aiming the flogger for her right buttock, and make contact. A thumping sound emits. She doesn't flinch. I do it again, this time to her left buttock, and then move around the back of her body, striking her harder as time passes. Little moans and gasps escape, and her buttocks and back turn the color of cherries, but no distress appears on her face. "Is it too much?"

"No," she says. I bring the tresses between her thighs again, trying to touch her pussy, making her groan and sigh. She thrusts her pelvis into the mattress. I take my fingers and touch her there. She's sopping wet. Restraint, flogging, and spankings sexually stimulate most women. Hell, it stimulates anyone, and doing it to women, especially this one, stimulates me. There's an energy exchange between us: I give, she receives, and then she sends it back to me.

I undo my belt and shove my pants to the floor. Usually, I'd strike the woman with my belt too, but until I learn more about those scars, I dare not. I climb on top of her, straddling her, and reach down between her ass and thighs and pet her with my hand, moving toward the mattress as she strains against the chains. Her pulsing pussy thrusts against my fingers. I lift her lower torso enough to bring my head between her legs, then find her delicious clit and lick and suck up her juices. I nip her clit before retrieving one of my vibrators. I touch it with the toy, then move it away, then bring it back, over and over, increasing her need. I shimmy to the bottom of the bed and place love bites all over her rear as she moves back and forth and tries to move away, but she can't, because the chains bind her to my bed. "Cruz, please," she cries.

"That's not how I asked to be addressed," I tease, dangling the flogger between her legs again and stroking her pussy with the handle while she moans, trying to move towards it.

"Please, Master, let me cum."

I climb to her head and bring my head to her ear. "You know what I want, but you have to want the same thing."

"I do. I do. Please, I—"

"Please, what? What do you want, Seven?"

"I need you inside of me. I'm burning. Help me…" She thrusts her ass against me.

"I believe you do. You almost came when I sucked you."

"No one has done it like that," she says, holding her head up from the mattress, her eyes melting and softening.

"It's like you said, then. I have magic powers, yes?"

"Yes," she smiles. "You do, Master."

I burst with happiness inside, move to the foot of the bed, unsnap the chains holding her feet, then to the top of the bed and unsnap her wrists. "Come to the side of the bed, turn on your back, and spread your legs. And ask the right way, Seven."

"Are you going to wear a condom?"

"I do with the others, but not tonight with you."

"But what if—"

"There is no if. You told me you couldn't have children the last time you were here. Was that a lie?"

"No, the truth."

"I have one question for you. Who gave you the scars on your back?"

"Jack, my husband," River says, looking away from me.

"With what?"

"A rattan cane."

"I thought so. Is that why you were frightened?"

"Yes, but not now."

"You didn't seem afraid of the crop the other day."

"I had my clothes on. I knew it wouldn't hurt too badly, and I knew you wouldn't hit my back."

Thank you for sharing that with me. The time for questions and long conversations is over. Now, ask for your desire the right way."

"Please, Master, fuck me," she says, her face flushed, legs open.

It's like the sun has shone on my being. I'm going to fuck River, something I've wanted even before she came back. My need increases every day I think of her. She waits to receive me. "Open wider," I say, standing on the floor in front of her, staring at her thighs, round belly, and pink pussy. I pin her down on the mattress first, laying her out, knowing she's mine. River tries to grab onto me. I share her desperation, too; my body is like hers. But I move her hands away.

"I need you," River says again.

"I'll decide when and how, not you." I slide my hands under her ass, lift her hips off the bed, and bring her pussy up to my cock. Wet and warm with more of her juices, it welcomes me, and within seconds, my cock reaches almost to the bottom of her. I plunge in deeper, and she encompasses me, arching her back and closing her eyes. "Keep your eyes on me," I say. "I need to watch you. " River isn't vocal like the other women in the house, who Dom from the bottom, requesting this and that and telling me exactly how to get them off, until I have to silence them. I have to guess what River likes by watching and listening.

I bring myself out of her and back in, toying with her, and she opens her legs wider, letting me know she wants more. She responds with a gasp when I fill her again. I watch her watch me, possibly the only one I've let do that, besides Gloria, but I didn't really have a choice with her. I need River to know that, without question, I own her, or at least I will when I deposit my essence into her and make her cum.

Still, like some women, she might not cum without some clitoral stimulation. You don't have a successful sex business without learning how to get people off. I have another toy set aside for her on the pillow. This vibrator uses sonic waves to induce multiple orgasms. I'm going to change Ms. Two Orgasms' life—or is it now three? I flick the pink miracle worker on and place it on her clit, and when I do, River's eyes open wider. She rocks right and left, attempting to escape her sweet pain as I continue thrusting my cock into her, bringing and taking the vibrator away.

"Ahh!" she screams a minute later. "I'm going to cum! Oh my God!" I lock eyes with her. Suddenly, she grabs ahold of my ass, her nails gouging into me as she pulls me towards her. I've only had one woman get rough with me, and she's not on this earth anymore.

River doesn't know I've held back with her, but once she scratches me like this, I slam in harder and move her calves higher on either side of my shoulders to fuck her deeper. I go faster and harder. A woman's tits during spirited fucking, I think, are like the joyful bounces of a child at play, and I get lost in their beauty. I want to make them bounce even harder, along with the rest of her. The noise of my balls hitting her ass and the bed squeaking is like heavy metal music, but I see delight instead of fear on her face as I get rougher. Her head tips back, and a smile appears.

"You want it harder, River?" I ask.

"Ahhh..."

"That's not an answer." Her cunt squeezes me, her muscles gripping. I stop moving.

"Please..." she cries.

"Tell me how you want it, slave."

"Harder, Master," she says.

"Rougher, you mean? Say it."

"Rougher, Master."

I laugh. I wouldn't have thought my shy River would be a fan of something I enjoy in bed, too. I slam into her, wondering if she knows what she's asking for and whether she can handle me. "Yes! Yes, yes!" she screams as I fuck her harder.

The bed moves in unison with us, hitting the wall whenever I plow into her. I should've turned on music to mask the sounds. She moans and lifts her hips higher. I'm giving her everything I've got, hitting the wall of her pussy until she clenches down. "Cruz… I mean, Master," she calls out, her eyes full of confusion.

"You have permission to cum," I say raggedly. "Cum on my dick. Think of a magical purpose for the energy you're about to disperse into the universe." Her pussy grips my cock as she thrashes into me, orgasming. I watch her lose herself and fall apart, her lips open, her eyes rolled up towards the back of her head, her forehead dotted with moisture. Suddenly, it's over for her. A look of embarrassment appears, and her eyes seem to change as she pulls away from me. Guilt, loss, and sadness seep into her face, and I don't want that for her. I bend over her and kiss her mouth. Our tongues intertwine. I explore her mouth and kiss her ear. "You're so beautiful, River," I whisper, and her eyes light up when I say her real name. I start on her again, slowly slipping in and out of her wetness, picking up the tempo, continuing to drive in softly but firmly. Finally, with one last thrust, I spill my heat into her and send my own intention into the universe, but this time it has nothing to do with cosmic change. *I want River forever.*

The thought makes me panic. I hadn't expected this kind of lovemaking from someone who spoke of trouble orgasming and awful marriages. I've used intimacy to connect our minds and bodies, combining masculine and feminine energy. I stare at

River's face, wanting to stay lost in those blue eyes that look up, admiring me. And I realize the trouble I'm in. I disengage immediately. I can't become more attached, so I do something that, even by my standards, is cold. I pull out of her and point to the mat on the floor. "Now clean yourself and go to your bed."

14

JUST FRIENDS

RIVER

"What have I done?" I ask myself, staring at my reflection in the bathroom mirror.

Suddenly, my reflection changes into the red-haired woman with angry eyes and rotting skin. "Stupid cow!" It's not my voice. "You can't trust Cruz; didn't I tell you that? Hurt him now, while you have the chance." Her tongue slithers out of her mouth like a snake. Then she's gone, and only the odor of roses remains, and it's my reflection back in the mirror, not hers. I wipe my tears, wash and dry my face, brush my teeth, clean, and dress. When I return to the room, Cruz is gone. I've made a big mistake.

I've had a crush on Cruz since the first day I met him. We were friends, or at least I thought we were. How silly to believe I could be friends with Cruz MacKenzie.

Gia and the others warned me, but I didn't listen, thinking I was different. I'm not different. I'm like the hundreds or maybe thousands he's had before. I could have said no, but I didn't, because deep down I wanted him and all his twisted thoughts. I hadn't expected he would push me away so quickly, though. I must have disappointed him. I have little experience. Twice with boys I didn't like, who probably didn't like me, who I snuck away with behind my mother's back. I let them touch me so I could know what other girls seemed to know, but I got nothing from those experiences, or my two marriages. One who couldn't...and another who only touched me to hurt me. Cruz made me feel something, and then he pushed me away.

After washing and dressing, I go to my children's room. They're playing a game with Gia. Gia's eyes meet mine, and I can tell by how she looks at me that she knows what's happened. "Guys, how about I get you ready for bed tonight?" Gia asks them, lowering her eyes, not wanting to read my sadness.

I return to Cruz's room, lie on the mat by the empty bed, and watch the snowfall in the dark. Little flakes kiss the glass, and I watch them drift away into the blackening night as I do.

Beep, beep, beep, beep, beep, beep.

"For God's sake, Seven, turn that off," Cruz grumbles from his bed.

I grab my new phone frantically from the mat next to me and turn the alarm off. I don't remember setting it.

"Get my coffee. Remember, strong and black."

I hustle to my feet and walk toward the bathroom, clutching my throbbing head, another headache.

"Stop," he calls out. "Where are you going?"

"To the bathroom, to dress."

"I didn't tell you to dress. I didn't give you clothes." He points to the door. "Get my coffee now."

"But I'm not—"

"I know what you are." His lips curl downwards. "No one cares if you're dressed or not, except you, of course."

"But my children—"

"You needn't worry. Gia's taken them out for breakfast, and then she's taking them to the zoo. Stop stalling," he says, a satisfied look spreading, knowing he'd swatted my excuses away.

My body shivers as I enter the hall. In winter, the house is always cold in the mornings. I tiptoe to the stairs, holding onto the twisted wood banister, praying no one else is awake. Most weekends, people sleep in, except for Gia and Bones, but Gia is out. I arrive in the kitchen and already smell coffee brewing. I run to the cupboard, find Cruz's special Day of the Dead mug, and pour the coffee in. I spin around and rush to the stairs, climbing each rung hurriedly without spilling a drop. I enter Cruz's bedroom. He's sitting with his back against a pile of pillows, with one hand behind his head. I present the coffee to him. "Where's the newspaper?" he asks, taking the coffee and settling into the pillows.

"You didn't ask for the paper," I respond as he takes a sip of his coffee.

"Not strong enough, slave," Cruz says. "You can bring the paper back when you go make another pot. Try again." He passes the mug back with a smirk.

"Please, don't make me go there again, I—"

"Hush. 'Master' is my title. You did it once, you can do it again. Now go." He points to the door.

"But what if someone sees me?"

"All the girls have walked around the house naked. You can too."

"I'm not comfortable—"

Cruz scowls. "Why do we continue to go over the same terrain? I don't care about your comfort. *My* comfort is what you need to consider. You do what I tell you. Fresh coffee, strong and black, and the newspaper." He picks up his phone, dismissing me.

RIVER

I arrive in the kitchen, throw the other coffee away, and clean the pot. I find espresso beans, grind them, and place them in the filter. I select "strong" on the brew dial and press start. Crazy noises emit from the two-thousand-dollar machine. I drink tea, so maybe I don't understand. Even my husband wouldn't spend that much on a coffee maker, but the last time I was here, Cruz explained that coffee was fuel and kept everyone going. He said he'd never scrimp on something so important.

I scan the kitchen table for the newspaper, but it's missing. I tiptoe into the great room, but again, nothing. I walk to the front door, thinking it might be outside. My mother once said a newspaper left close to the door will keep the spirits out because "they have to count every word." If that's true, I should leave it outside of Cruz's room, because I think his room is haunted. I open the door a crack. The cold air makes me shiver, but of course, it would, I'm not wearing a stitch of clothing. The front porch is empty.

I hear coughing noises behind me. I panic, turning around quickly, and slam the door. Bones snickers as his eyes travel my body. "You're probably looking for this," he says, holding the newspaper out to me. As I grasp for it, he snatches my wrist and draws me to him, holding me tight as I struggle to get away. "Cruz likes to play games with his slaves. Do you like to play, River?"

I finally shake myself loose from Bones's grasp, still holding my prize, and run up the staircase as fast as I can until I'm standing in front of Cruz's door. I realize I don't have his coffee, but I can't go back with Bones down there. I enter and close the heavy door behind me.

Cruz is on the phone talking with someone, but I only hear the end. "If we're going to be in bed together, I guess this is one way to establish trust, but I don't like—" He sees me. "We'll talk later. I have another call." Cruz puts the phone away and motions me over, scowling at my hands. As I hand him the *Tribune*, he asks, "Where's my coffee?"

"Umm, I couldn't bring any."

"What do you mean?" His head tilts to one side; his eyes narrow.

"Bones was there."

"So what?" Cruz asks, staring at me with a sour expression.

"I couldn't."

"You can and you will," he blurts out. "Go back and get my coffee."

"No," I say.

"You're refusing to obey?" he asks, becoming speechless for a few seconds. "And you didn't call me Master, either."

"I guess I am, and I guess I didn't."

"You prefer punishment?"

"I guess I do."

"You give your consent?" he asks in an incredulous tone, shaking his head and clenching one fist briefly.

"Yes, Master."

Cruz climbs out of bed, his hair loose. He's only wearing black biker shorts as he takes long strides over to the throne and sits. He points to his lap. "Lay over my lap, Seven, and let me warn you; defy me this time, and the punishment will be more severe."

I don't move.

Cruz glares and continues, "Do I need to call Bones to help me?"

I'm losing my mind. Anxiety cruises through me. When I get near enough, Cruz grabs me and flips me over his lap so that my bangs touch the floor, my head faces his ankles, and my rear the ceiling. I go into a trance-like state, maybe because too much blood travels to my brain too quickly, or maybe because I'm in shock.

There's no warning. Cruz's hand comes fast on my ass—*slap, slap, slap, slap, slap.*

There are five of them, each harder than the last, and their sting takes my breath away.

He flips me up and pushes me towards the floor, forcing me to land on my rear. Cruz looms over me and sneers, "Are you ready to get my coffee now?"

"No, Cruz, I'm not." This time, I use his real name on purpose. Nothing Cruz can do can make me go back down there again and face Bones.

"Seems someone's woken on the wrong side of the bed." Cruz walks towards the cage in the corner of the room. He unlatches it and motions for me to get in. "You can spend some time in here, consider your actions, and decide if it was worth it. Crawl, slave."

Cruz goes about his business, showering and dressing after I'm locked inside. He puts his overcoat on, goes to his refrigerator, brings out bottles of water, and places them close enough that I can reach through the metal bars and pull them through.

"I'll be gone all day. I have appointments. Bones will bring you lunch and let you out for bathroom breaks. Maybe you'll grow accustomed to him." Cruz smirks, turns his back, walks to the thermostat, pushes the control up a couple of degrees, and leaves.

15

CAGED

RIVER

I sip the water but haven't eaten breakfast, and my stomach growls. I follow the light and shadows as they travel across the floor, and try to understand what's happening, what could happen in the future, and how I can prepare. I don't know how much time has passed, but I've drunk two bottles of water and need to pee soon. I've had to go for the last hour, and my discomfort becomes unbearable, *like many times before.*

I also don't want Bones to come. I don't want whoever it is to see me. The door squeaks open and shuts, then I hear soft footsteps. I know they're not Cruz's; he wears boots, and they make a tapping noise when he walks. I curl myself into a tight ball.

"I have your lunch, and Cruz wants you to stretch your legs and go to the bathroom, so you gotta come out." Even if I didn't recognize his voice, I'd recognize his baggy pants and Nike high-tops. The crate unlocks, the gate opens, and he waits.

"I don't need to go. I'm not hungry," I say.

"Doesn't matter. Cruz says you gotta, so you gotta."

I know better than to not listen. Bones will pull me out if I don't come out by myself. I get on all fours and back out of the cage. When I see a metal tag with a Doberman's imprint, I realize Cruz is keeping me in a dog crate, and my heart breaks. It's stupid because what's the difference between a cage and a crate? But either is preferable to being locked in a closet in the dark and beaten, like Jack used to do to me.

I can barely stand, and I hobble to the bathroom, my body stiff from folding myself into the small space and lying on the ground with only slight padding in the cold room. I'm ready to close the door when Bones calls out, "Cruz says the bathroom door has to stay open."

I sit on the toilet, but nothing happens. I'm so nervous I can't relieve myself. I see Cruz's robe on the floor, slip into it, and try again. A stream of pee jets out of me.

When I come out of the bathroom, Bones points at the robe. "Cruz won't like that. When you get back in the crate, take the robe off." Then he motions at the desk. "Your lunch is there." I'm starving but comforted by having the robe. I sit at the desk and wolf down the sandwich as Bones studies my every move. "I can help you," he says after I finish the sandwich.

"How?"

"Make it so you're not a slave."

How will Bones do that? "What about Cruz?" I ask. "He won't let me stop until he's ready."

"He could disappear, you never know," Bones says.

Did Cruz tell Bones to say that? Is this a test? "What would happen to me around here if I'm not a slave?"

Bones walks over and touches my head. "I'm sure we can work something out."

I toss my head out of his reach and scoot the chair away from him. "What would happen to my children?" I ask.

"I promise they'll be fine," Bones says.

I walk back to the crate and kneel to crawl back in. "Take the robe off," Bones says. I stand and drop the robe to the floor and crawl back into the crate.

"You don't want to live like this for a year, do you, River?" Bones asks, latching and locking the crate. He picks the robe from the floor, returns it to the bathroom, collects the plate from the desk, and moves to the doorway. "Think about it." And he leaves.

I consider his question. Can I do this for a year? I never know what to expect and how it will go with Cruz. Yesterday, I'd never felt so appreciated. The way his tongue explored my mouth, his hands searching my body, and his cock pressing into my pussy. For the first time, I enjoyed what I did with someone. But afterward, he pushed me away.

Being with Cruz is like a rollercoaster ride. He kisses me like someone who knows, enjoys, and cares about what he's doing, not going through the motions. I scroll through images of Cruz in my mind and roll myself into a ball again. I close my eyes until I hear my children's voices next door, making them spring open. I pray Bones' locked the door and that they can't enter. I worry until the room darkens, turns black, and their voices disappear.

I hear banging, and the cold air hits my body. Someone has opened the window in the bathroom next to the crate. The wind howls again, and the window closes. Whispers again, and the water turns on in the bathroom. I call out, "Master, is that you?" The water turns off, but there's no answer. I lose myself in worries and anxiety.

Light blinds me. I've been in the dark too long and must have fallen asleep. Cruz's footsteps cross the floor. He unlocks and opens the crate and crouches down by my ear. "You're going to need a hot bath. It's cold in here. Give me a moment."

I realize I need to use the toilet badly, and if I don't go soon, I'll pee myself, but Cruz hasn't given permission. I don't know how much time has passed, but I can't hold it anymore. "I need to go to the bathroom," I call out.

Cruz's footsteps echo through the room again. "By this time, you should know the proper way to ask." This time he's standing at the back of the crate.

"Master, I need to use the bathroom, please."

"You have permission. Go."

I back out of the crate and head to the lavatory, moving as quickly as I dare. I know better than to close the door, so I sit on the toilet with my arms wrapped around myself, but nothing comes. I've held myself so long, I can't go. I strain, but again my body gives nothing. Several more minutes pass, and the pain is excruciating. Cruz steps into the bathroom and somehow knows my problem. He turns the spigot on at the sink, and the sound of running water gets me started. My urine slowly trickles out of me, then comes faster and keeps coming and coming. The pain lessens. I pee for over a minute.

Cruz checks the bathroom window, slams it shut, and locks it. "Who opened the window?" he asks.

"I don't know, maybe the wind."

Cruz grunts. "I locked it," is all he says, and he walks closer. "How many times did Bones let you out?" he asks, uncrossing his arms and leaning down, his eyebrows raised.

"Once."

Cruz steps back. "Unacceptable," he growls. His nostrils flare, and his blonde hair comes unloose from his man bun as he takes wide steps out of the bathroom. Seconds later, the bedroom door slams. I return to the bedroom and put my head against the wood-paneled door. I hear Cruz lecturing Bones in the hallway. "You had specific instructions. I said to let her out at least every two hours. And who opened the bathroom window? The room is freezing."

"Ahhh, I had some interruptions, distractions, but—"

Thumping and crashing sounds interrupt Bones' explanation. I back away from the door. A few minutes later, Cruz returns, holding his hand and rubbing his bleeding knuckles. He strides towards me, angry. "Come with me," he barks, and takes my arm and pulls my still unclothed body into the bathroom. He lets go of me to turn on the shower. He undresses himself and holds the shower door open. "Get in," he orders and then follows me.

Cruz pours shampoo into his hand. "Lean your head back." I know better than to argue, especially when his eyes are flashing, and his jaw clenches like that. Cruz starts at my temples, then rubs the soap into the back of my scalp and massages my head over and over. It surprises me how relaxed I've become with Cruz's hands touching me. He retrieves the shower massager from the holder. "Close your eyes," he says, and rinses the soap out of my hair. "I'm sorry for leaving you all day. It won't happen again. Whether you get punished again is in your hands, depending on your behavior, but I'm never trusting your care to another again." He squeezes shower gel all over a giant loofah and scrubs my back, breasts, arms, and legs until my skin turns pink. "Spread your legs," he says. He squeezes more shower gel into his hand and presses it between my legs, cleaning me. His hands are gentle. As he rinses the soap away, his lips shoot upward and his eyes open wide. He adjusts the spray on the shower massager.

"This is another way," he says, and brings the shower massager towards my pussy, pressing my back against the tiled shower. With his other hand, he spreads my folds, exposing my clit, then sprays it with the powerful stream of water. I both want to get away from what he's doing and rush towards the water spray. I make no decision, and in less than a minute, I'm bucking my hips into space as Cruz's eyes dance with mine. "We've added to your count," he grins. "Is this number five, River? Or have you given yourself more that I don't know about?"

I don't answer him. After that, things get more intimate, but not in a way that I want.

CRUZ

River's sitting on the bed, still nude. I haven't told her to dress, and she hasn't tried to. It takes time to take away defenses and shape someone, but less for some.

"I'd like a cup of coffee, River." Her eyes meet mine, and they waver for a second or two, a faraway look again, before standing and walking towards the door. I let her go as far as the staircase before calling her back. "I've changed my mind. We don't have time."

My heart aches, knowing her faraway eyes are my fault, and that she didn't tell me no. Now, there's no way I can tell Angelo I'm canceling tonight because my slave disobeyed and requires punishment.

I didn't like having to cage her like some kind of dog. River's my pet, it's true, but it doesn't mean Bones, or anyone else, has the license to abuse her. Bones' excuses are bullshit. He wants her to suffer. Why else would he not let her out and leave the window open? Even though he swears he didn't. Slaves' suffering is not off the table, but I have different things and reasons in mind. River will hopefully find some pleasure in what I do.

I forced River to confront five of her fears: appearing naked in front of others, getting close to Bones, being flogged, being restrained, and being contained. But the most significant success was her having the courage to stand up to me and refuse to fetch my coffee this morning. It's unfortunate I had to punish her for it.

Bringing her off with the shower massager, her skin aglow from the hot water, scrubbing her, the look in her eyes when she came—I can't get enough of it.

After I got her off, I shaved her. She tried to argue, but I shut her down, insisting it was my preference, and she gave in. I should have told her the truth.

Tonight's a test for both of us. Will River obey? If she does, she'll lose all respect for me.

But I'll get her out of my system, and she won't have a hold on me anymore.

River's quiet now. Her face is unreadable. Did she enjoy what I did to her in the shower? She seemed to. I wanted to shove my cock into her and hold her tight, but I didn't. I need to maintain my distance. I pull her dress from my closet and place the garment in her hands. "I need a bra and panties," she says, her eyes inquisitive.

"You don't need them."

"But I want them and I—"

"Put the dress on. Concern yourself with what I want." I turn my back.

RIVER

"Gia, come to my room and bring your makeup kit," Cruz says into his cell. A few minutes later, there's a tap at the door.

"You look lovely, River," Gia says, entering.

"Put some mascara on her and do anything else she needs," Cruz says, moving to the hallway.

Gia places her makeup kit on Cruz's desk. I sit in the chair, and Gia comes closer, then stops. "Where did you get that?" she asks, pointing at my necklace.

"Cruz gave it to me," I say.

Her face looks angry, but she turns away, gets mascara out of her case, and comes back to me, her anger gone. She brushes the mascara on my lashes. Her eyes travel to my earrings, and she stares at them. "You should wear your hair away from your face if you wear those. I'll style your hair if you like."

Cruz says as he enters the room with Alex and Joy, "I want her hair the way it is." Gia keeps quiet, taking out the lipstick next. "Too dark," he says, looking at the colors. "Light or mauve pink will go with her coloring."

"Mommy, you look like a princess," Joy says.

"Are you sure you're my mom?" Alex says suspiciously, his eyes narrow.

Cruz walks towards the closet. He returns, takes a cashmere wrap, and places it around my shoulders. As I grasp the ends, I hear Gia gasp. "What?" Cruz asks.

"The wrap is beautiful," she says, but I notice Gia's staring at the bracelets on my wrists, not the wrap. "Anything else?" she asks him.

"No, you can go."

Gia hugs me, closes her case, and leaves me with Cruz and the children.

16
BOGO

CRUZ

I remove a favorite toy from my pocket while we're in the back seat of the car, my quietest vibrator, which contains two parts. I play a game with the others with it; one of them always wears it when we go out, and the rest don't know which one it is. They enjoy guessing who's wearing it, and the people around us are unaware of what's going on. "Open your legs, Seven."

River stares at my hand. She can never hide her emotions. She freezes with her hand at her throat. Adorable. "No, please, Master, don't make—"

"Hush. Push your dress up." I help her, my hand becoming lost in the layers of organza until feeling warm, soft flesh. I position the vibrator, attach the belt around her waist that holds it in place, check the Bluetooth on my phone, and turn the power to low. I watch her shift in her seat, eyes expanding and mouth dropping open.

"I can't," she says, moving. "I can't wear this the whole time. No way."

"Fine. Wear it during the appetizer. Before the entrée, excuse yourself, go to the restroom, and remove it." I lower my voice and press my lips against her ear so my crew can't hear. "Lick the toy clean with your tongue, place it in your purse, return to the table, and give me a loving kiss, so I can taste you too." *Will she punch me?*

"What?" She wrinkles her brow and shakes her head. "I refuse. You can't make me."

"True, I can't; and you forgot to call me Master again. I assure you you're missing a chance to have fun."

"How?" she asks, a small smile forming.

"You can't do anything to disclose you're wearing it. It's quite a challenge. I bet you can't do it."

"I don't know…" Her brow wrinkles.

"You'd probably make too much noise or cum while you're sitting with everyone. If people figure out you have it, then I'd have to—"

"Punish me?" Her expression isn't fearful but eager.

"Yes. What punishment would you like? I'm curious."

River closes her eyes for a second. "Another spanking with your hand," she says, her eyes excited.

"You liked the last one?" I ask. "It was supposed to punish you, not pleasure you."

"Maybe. It was a little of both."

"Obviously, you enjoyed it, or you wouldn't be asking for another." I shake my head and chuckle. "So, your choice of wearing the toy, yes or no?"

"I'm not sure. Ahh…I guess."

"Good girl. I knew you weren't a coward." Since she wants another spanking, I'll accommodate. We arrive at the restaurant, and one of my crew members opens the car door for us, but before I can climb out, River springs something on me.

"When Bones brought me lunch, he offered to help me. Says you might not be in the picture much longer."

I wave my hand to dismiss the idea. Is this a ploy to create a division between a crew member and me? I have a surprise for her, too, and I can't put off telling her any longer. River's the part that seals my deal, the free bonus after Angelo pays maximum for everything else.

We stop in the lobby. I pull River aside from my two men and hold her hand. "Remember the part in the contract that discusses sharing you with someone else?"

She meets my gaze. "Yes." Her eyes shift back and forth.

"I have a colleague. You'll meet him tonight. Unless you have a problem with him, you'll be having sex with him. His name's Angelo. But you won't be alone. I'll be there. I'm doing the same with his wife."

"And if I have a problem? Then what?" she asks, her voice flat, pulling her hand away.

"We'll discuss your feelings. But remember, I covered the matter in the contract which you signed." She places one of her hands over the other and looks back at the doorway like she wants to bolt. "Don't even think about it," I growl.

"I'm not. You said I'd have to consent," River says, looking me in the eyes. "It seems too soon."

"You do have to consent, and I can't force you. I decide when it should happen, though. What's the reason you don't wish to comply?"

"I don't want to."

"Are you sure? Or are you afraid, like you were with the flogger? Or are you concerned with what other people think, like you were when you walked through the house naked? Let's go to the table, and you can meet him. Try to remember it's what I want." I take her hand and lead River into the private dining room.

Angelo is at the table, but his wife is nowhere in sight. I check my phone and increase the vibrator's intensity. As soon as Angelo sets his eyes on River, he can't take them away. River's cheeks flush, and she stumbles as she shakes hands with him, the vibrator getting to her. She directs her eyes to the floor out of embarrassment, not because of anything I'd taught her, but Angelo would never know that.

"Where's Joanna?" I ask Angelo.

"A change in plans. Joanna's at home, getting prepared. She's looking forward to our night together. Perhaps we can hurry our dinner along," he says, staring at River and licking his lips. "You know women."

"Excuse my manners; Angelo, this is Seven, the one I spoke of."

"Oh yes, the slave." Angelo comes forward. "Cruz, you have good taste. Her face is beautiful. This one is like the necklace she wears, a rare, raw pearl. You might only find such a jewel once in a lifetime." Angelo kisses her hand. *Why didn't she pull away?*

"Let's sit," he continues. "The wait staff won't disturb us. I know them all well."

I take my chair, and River stands by my side, waiting for my direction.

"She's well trained. I'm impressed. My wife and I want a slave. She'd be a lovely one, if you ever decide to get rid of her."

"What do you think, Seven?" I ask. "Would you want to become a slave to a man and a woman, a couple?" I hope she tells me to go to hell so I can get us out of here. This is all starting to go wrong.

"Whatever pleases you," River says, not looking up.

Angelo claps his hands. "My God, she's an angel. Agrees with everything you say. I have to get one of these."

"Sit on Angelo's lap," I say. The humiliation will have her racing for the exit. Angelo scoots his chair out, allowing room for her to slip in. His face beams when she lowers herself to his lap. I take the phone and change the tempo of the vibrator, watching River bite her lips and choke down sounds. Her face grows redder, and she twists her hands.

My stomach turns as my fingers tighten on the phone.

"You're a pretty one," Angelo coos, running his hand on her arm as she squirms, attempting to avoid both him and the pulsating vibrator. He leans over to me and asks, "May I touch her anywhere else, or is it off-limits until later?"

"As long as she consents, you can touch." River's eyes meet mine. "Seven, did you hear what I said? You need to consent."

She shrugs. "Yes, sure, why not?" *What's wrong with her?*

"Hold up," I say to Angelo as his hands move underneath her dress. "Let's enjoy our meal first. Seven hasn't eaten today. Let's save all of this until your house." I motion for River to sit in the seat next to me.

"You're right, my friend; food first," Angelo says. His eyes are disappointed as he watches her leave his lap and go to the chair. He lowers his voice and covers his mouth with the edge of his hand. "Her skin is soft, like satin. I'm sure even softer between her legs, yes?"

"Yes, you made your preference known." River stares at me again, but her eyes are filled with hate this time. She understands now why I insisted on shaving her after our shower together.

"Would you gentlemen like me to pour the champagne?" one of the wait staff interrupts.

"Yes," Angelo says, and I nod my head. "She drinks, yes?" Angelo asks me.

"Of course. River drinks and eats what I tell her to."

The server places a glass of champagne in front of River. She waits for me. "How cute," Angelo says. "She's delaying her enjoyment until you taste yours.

How do you like?" Angelo asks River after I gave her permission to drink.

"Delicious," she says and takes another sip.

Angelo beams, drinking from his own flute. "People don't realize champagne is more dangerous to drink than hard liquor."

"True," I say, drinking from my glass.

"The bubbles take the intoxication through the bloodstream and to your head faster than anything else. If I want to bed a woman, this works better than any aphrodisiac." He chuckles. "Especially when they learn I spent a thousand dollars a bottle for it. Money, it seems, is an aphrodisiac too."

River places her still-full glass on the table. I retrieve my phone and increase the vibrator's power.

"Ohhhh!" she screams out, flapping her hand and knocking over both her champagne and mine.

"Don't worry," Angelo says, believing her cries are over the spilled drink. He signals one of the wait staff over. They remove our glasses and clean off the table. River smirks while I attempt to dry my pants off with my dinner napkin. *Did she do it on purpose?*

After I'm done drying off, I increase the vibrator's power using my phone again. River bites her lips and wraps her hands around herself. She shifts in her seat, first one way and then another, arches her back, tilts her head towards the ceiling, and then brings her chin down, fighting against an impending orgasm. I'd get to spank her if she does. Before I can decide what to do, her hand appears from underneath the table, and she dumps the still-whirring vibrator onto my lap.

"Your turn," she whispers. "Stick it up your—"

"Would anyone like to have another glass?" Angelo interrupts, holding the bottle and pointing to our fresh glasses.

"No, thank you," River says while I shake my head. I pick up my phone from the table and pretend I'm looking at messages, turn the app off, reach down, take the vibrator, face River, pretend to lick it, and place it in my pocket as River's eyes challenge mine.

Angelo continues eating his oysters, totally unaware of what's occurred.

She fought back. I like that she did.

River doesn't make eye contact with either of us for the rest of the meal, nor speaks. She's become a piece of furniture, like I once described to her, a slave should be. After Angelo and I have coffee and dessert, and he fields several calls from his wife, we leave the restaurant with our entourage.

***

Back in the car, River finally cracks. "Please, Master, reconsider." She grabs onto my hand.

"We discussed this. If you're loyal to me, you'll obey," I say, keeping my emotions under wraps.

"There must be another way, please—"

"Do you find Angelo distasteful?"

"Yes. This whole evening is distasteful."

"Why?" I ask.

"I don't love him."

She'd expressed her thoughts about intimacy the first time she stayed with me. Old-fashioned ones about loving someone before you had sex with them. Yet, she married a husband who didn't love her, and now—

"Of course you don't. You just met him. But you don't have to. It can just be fun sex. You don't need to feel guilty for taking pleasure. Sex is part of nature. It's natural to have sexual desire."

"Maybe that philosophy works for you."

I continue my argument. "You fucked me. You don't love *me*, do you?"

Her face instantly changes from panic to confusion. "Actually...I do." River's hand squeezes mine.

"What are you saying?"

"You should care for the person you have sex with. I don't care for Angelo, but I do care for you."

"You can't."

"Why not?" she asks as she peeks at me.

"I've hurt you, and I'm going to hurt you even more. You're smarter than this."

"But why are you hurting me? Especially when—"

"Because I enjoy it."

"This isn't you. Where's the other you? Where's the Cruz from months ago, the one I shared with, who cares and listens?"

"He isn't real, Seven. I pretended to be what you wanted me to be. This is the real me."

She shakes her head vehemently. "I don't believe that. You have a choice which Cruz you're going to be. If you're the one I know is real, then you love me too, and you'd never hurt me on purpose. If you choose to be the pretend one and act like you don't care, you'll give me to Angelo."

"What you're failing to understand right now is that I'm your Master, not Cruz," I say with what feels like desperation in my voice. "And you're not River, you're...you're my slave." I frown and slump back into my seat. Goddamnit. River still believes in Prince Charming.

As we approach Angelo's driveway, I tap my driver's shoulder. "Get us out of here, back to The Palace." *Fuck, I am Prince Charming.*

"Are you sure?" Tito asks, incredulously.

"Do what I tell you to do, drive." *Since I am Prince Charming, I have to get her out of this.*

Ring ring. I know who it is before I pick it up. "What's going on?" Angelo screams. "You pull in my drive and then turn around and leave? My wife's looking forward to this." His anger echoes through the car, even though I don't have the cell on speakerphone.

"I understand you're disappointed, and your wife too. But I don't wish to do this at the moment."

"How can we be in business together if I can't trust you to follow through?"

"That's your choice," I say.

"There will be repercussions," Angelo says. "Maybe not today, nor tomorrow, but some day you will pay for this insult."

I disconnect the call. River and I don't talk until we are almost back to The Palace. "I'm sorry for ruining your deal," River says.

"Be quiet, slave. You ruined nothing. My decision had nothing to do with you. It was for me."

When we enter The Palace, Bones has an ice pack on his face. "What's going on?" he asks, rising from the couch. "I didn't expect you back so early."

"Nothing. The deal with Angelo is off. Triple security on all our houses."

Now I have both Angelo and River's husband to worry about.

Bones doesn't respond fast enough to my demand and continues to sit, undressing River with his eyes.

"Now! Do it now!" I bark, making Bones hustle from the room.

17

A WORLD OF PRAYERS

CRUZ

"Where are they?" River screams in my ear as she wakes me up out of a deep sleep. She straddles me, beating me with her fists. "What did you do with them?"

"What are you talking about?" I ask groggily, pushing her away as my head throbs, another headache.

"Joy and Alex are missing. They aren't in their beds. They're nowhere in the house. I kissed them goodnight after we got home last night, and now they're gone."

"Gia probably took them out for breakfast."

"No, Gia's here and so is everyone else," River whimpers. "Is this punishment because I didn't...please your friend, and refused you too?" Her voice is hoarse from yelling.

"I pulled the plug, not you. Angelo wasn't good enough for you. You think I'm so fragile I can't handle a woman saying no to me, slave? The truth is, you need to stand up for yourself more often."

"I had a dream last night that someone took them, and she said I couldn't have them back unless—"

"Yeah? And who took them in the dream?" I ask as I climb out of bed.

"I don't know who she was. The woman with jewels and red hair. The one I mentioned before. The one who smells like roses."

River's description causes me to stop. *Smells like roses.* Gloria wore a scent like that. It lingered in any room for hours, even if she wasn't in it.

I call Bones, but he says he hasn't seen the children since last night. I check my security tapes and notice the cameras are inactive and nothing's been recorded since early yesterday afternoon. I call the security company to find out more, but all they tell me is that the system is inactive and they'll schedule a service call as soon as possible.

We walk into the children's bedroom, then their bathroom, searching for anything out of place. I notice the window above the toilet is ajar. I look out and see someone has extended the fire escape ladder and moved it under the window, and snow is missing from some of the metal steps. The cold air hits me.

"Oh, my God. My husband," River says, looking over my shoulder, seeing the fire escape, then throwing herself in my arms.

"We don't know that." I hold her shoulders and make eye contact.

"I'll call him." River takes the phone out of her pocket.

I snatch it away. "You can't."

"Why not?"

"Because yours can only call one person, me." I pass her my cell. "If you want to try calling your husband, you can use mine."

She taps her husband's number into my phone and holds it to

her ear. Standing next to her, I hear the call go directly to voice-mail. "We are busy right now, so please leave a message, and we will...."

When the message beeps, she begins babbling, "Do you have them? Don't hurt them, please, I'll do anything you want—"

I snatch the phone away and push the "end call" button. "Never grovel to anyone, River."

She pulls herself together and paces throughout the room. "What should I do? Tell me, Cruz," she asks, latching onto me.

RIVER

Cruz says to get my coat, then walks me into my children's room. He pulls Joy's unicorn balloon by the string, dragging it from the frescoed ceiling covered with angels, and selects Alex's soldier figurine off the nightstand. I follow him as he walks through the house and out the back door. "I need to be with nature," he says, walking through naked trees hung with colorful bottles.

"What are these?" I ask, touching a blue bottle.

"Bottle wind chimes. If you have evil spirits, you place bottles on the bare branches of your trees. The evil spirits get trapped in the bottle and can't do you any harm. If you listen close you can hear them moaning." He points to the leafless trees. "The answer to everything is here, in the wind, in the water droplets from the snow and the clouds drifting above." We walk to the small gazebo, the snow crunching under our feet, climb the two steps, and enter. Cruz attaches the balloon to one of the gazebo posts and places the wooden soldier on the top stone of a makeshift altar he's built.

Cruz's eyes drift like he's meditating. He holds his hands out towards the altar, stepping inside the circle shape made with shells and stones, and says, "*Father Mars, I pray and ask thee to be gracious and merciful to me and my household; that thou ward off seen and unseen threats, ruin and unseasonable influence; and that thou permit my house to flourish and preserve my health and strength and those of my household. To this intent, Father Mars, please accept my offerings of a magical unicorn to ride, a soldier for your army, and my ring for lasting prosperity.*" *Cruz places his skull-butterfly ring in a brass bowl on the altar. He opens his wallet and places all his cash in the bowl, too, removes a lighter from his jacket, brushes his finger against it until a flame appears, and lights the contents. Orange flames jump, and black smoke drifts through the air.* "*We're protected against all evil, and the children will return safely,*" *he says to me. The flames curl the paper, blackening the silver, and the smoke floats away.*

"*How can you know that?*"

"*It's March 1, and this month is named after Father Mars. He knows our hearts are pure and strong, and that we're worth his time.*"

"*Who is Father Mars?*"

"One of the Roman gods. He's known for his military prowess and power. He'll help us."

"I'm going to pray too." I gaze towards the heavens as crows fly above me. I place my hands together. "Loving Father, touch me now with your healing hands, for I believe that your will is for me to be well in mind, body, soul, and spirit. Cover me with the most precious blood of your Son, our Lord Jesus Christ, from the top of my head to the soles of my feet. Cast anything that should not be in me. And I pray the same for Joy, Alex, and Cruz." I take Cruz's hand.

"That's a prayer I've heard many times before," he says. "But from your lips, I experienced peace instead of..." He shakes his head. "Thank you for including me in your prayer." He kisses my forehead and wraps his fingers tighter around my hand, warming my fingers and my heart.

"Yes, it's one of my favorites. I learned it in Catholic school. I said it last night too, when you—"

He sighs. "I'm sorry for my behavior. Your prayer must've worked, because I needed a way out."

"You said you did it for yourself."

"Yes...no. I didn't want you to do something that would hurt you, and sharing you, would have hurt both you and me." He stares into my eyes. "You're mine."

"Only for a year," I say, letting go of his hand.

"Yes, and I know it'll take a long time before you'll trust me again." Cruz brings me to him, bends his head, and makes our foreheads meet. "I vow I'll get Joy and Alex back, even if I have to sacrifice myself."

THE SNOW IS FALLING AGAIN, and it's late afternoon now. The two of us are in Cruz's room. He's even quieter than normal. It's dark except for a single candle. Cruz meditates while studying it. The only noise comes from the women preparing to leave for their assignments with members of Cruz's crew. Soft laughter, footsteps in the hall and on the steps, and then quiet. He looks away from the flame and turns to me. "Last night, you mentioned a conversation you had with Bones, and I dismissed what you said. I shouldn't have. Unlike most people, you don't tell lies to turn them into an advantage for yourself. I had a vision." He motions to the candle. "I saw him in the flame. Tell me again what Bones said exactly."

"I can't remember his specific words, but it's how I told it to you in the car; he alluded that you weren't always going to be the boss, and that he could help me. I wouldn't have to be a slave or perform like the others, and my children would be fine. All I had to do was cooperate. Pretty much that was the gist of it."

"Bone's isn't a risk-taker. He's always been jealous, but weak. He'd never have the balls to challenge me if he didn't have someone helping him. I told you before he wanted you, but it seems like he wants more, everything."

"How can you be sure it's him?" I ask.

"By setting a trap," Cruz says, taking the partially blackened skull and butterfly ring and threading a chain through the ring's opening. He places it over my neck. "This was my talisman. Now it's yours. It's been anointed with both of our fluids and charged in fire. It represents the change and the strength in both of us."

"Will it protect me from the voices? The woman who smells like roses?" I ask.

Cruz eyes me suspiciously. "I think it's time for me to hear exactly what these voices have been saying to you."

BAM BAM. Cruz grips my arm, pounding on Bones' door. "What?" Bones calls out, opening his door, his body stiffening when he sees it's Cruz, shoving his hands in his pockets, and acting nonchalant.

"I can't take another minute of her crying about her kids," Cruz says, pushing me towards him. "She's not working out as my slave, either. Wouldn't sleep with Angelo last night and ruined the deal with him. You take her." He shoves me again, this time into Bones' arms. "Put her on the hotel schedule tomorrow. Only our whales, though. She's fresh meat, and she'll fetch top dollar."

"Yeah, I've got a couple of guys in mind. They'll pay at least four grand. No problem." Bones grabs my arm and pulls me inside.

"No touching the goods until she earns for a couple of weeks," Cruz calls out. "Keep her on lockdown so she doesn't run, because with her kids gone, she might try." Cruz turns away and walks back to his room, leaving me with Bones.

"Don't worry," Bones says after closing the door. "I won't turn you out. I'll pretend to. We'll stay in the hotel room while the other girls earn and wait for them to finish."

"Cruz will never allow a shortage without some questions."

"Don't worry, I've got money to cover it. If he's still around by then."

"But my children. I need to find them."

Bones takes out his phone. "I'm going to show you something, but you've got to keep quiet." He turns on his phone. "They're safe." He flashes a short video of Alex and Joy playing in a room I don't recognize. *Cruz is right.*

"I want them back."

"Follow instructions and everything's going to work out," Bones says. "Let's get to know each other a little." He bends to kiss me, his hands cold as he brings me towards him. I move away, holding the dark skull ring now hanging between my breasts, causing Bones' lips to only graze my cheek. "You do want to keep them safe, right?" he asks, his eyes narrowing.

"You promised," I say.

"We both have promises to keep, yes?"

Is Cruz listening? I back away. *Love is dangerous, and I should run from both of them.*

"I'll go along when Alex and Joy are back in this house, not before. You had no right to take them away."

Bones comes closer and lowers his voice. "I had to. Cruz is going down tonight. You wouldn't want them in the house when it happens, would you?"

"Are you doing it?"

"No, someone else. I brought the security system down so they can come in. You not being in the room with him makes it easier. He'll be alone."

I pray Cruz can hear every word.

Bones walks closer, wrapping his arms around me tightly, causing my stomach to churn.

"Let's get better acquainted," he says, looking in my eyes as if deciding what he wants to do with me. "Unfortunately, we never got the opportunity the last time you were here. Always so skittish. But I'm sure Cruz has groomed you to handle more. Yes?"

"Umm, I'm not sure..."

"Come on, don't be coy. I don't want to bore you. Tell me what you've done. Have you worn a vibrator or had sex in public? Did he make you wear a butt plug while doing housekeeping chores? Did he use a ball gag or blindfold you? I bet he's edged you. Cruz edges all his slaves."

"He's done none of those things. What's edging?"

Bones laughs and rolls his eyes. "How can you not know? He fingers you or uses a vibrator, gets you all worked up repeatedly, but doesn't let you orgasm. Then he'll bind your hands so you can't bring yourself off. I've heard some of them yelling out loud, begging to cum. He'll let it go on for days."

"He wouldn't."

"All true. He's already made you walk around the house nude. I witnessed that firsthand. He even wanted you to have sex with Angelo. He's got a playlist. Most Doms do."

"What are you talking about?"

"Poor little River, such an innocent. Or naïve." He flattens me against the wall, the cold stone against my back making me shiver. "He took away your books, controls when you go to sleep and when you wake, won't let you wear clothes, locks you in a crate, and makes you watch when he fucked another woman."

"How do you know that?"

"The girls discuss what he does. Some of them would love to be in your shoes, but I think you don't like it much. The best you can hope for is that he tires of you. If you last more than a few months, you won't be the same. I've seen it happen. He has to find a new Master for 'em, because the girl can't think for herself anymore and wants to remain a slave. Do you want a new Master?"

"No."

"Then stay with me and give me what I want here." He points to the bed. "You do, and you're off the hook the rest of the time. No kneeling, no 'yes, Master, no Master' bullshit. I have simple tastes. I'm not like Cruz. I don't need the whips and chains to get off." *I don't want simple; I want Cruz.*

Is Bones telling the truth? Would Cruz tire of me, and I'd be a slave forever, only to someone else? I run my fingers around the skull ring, and it comforts me, like Cruz said it would.

"Blowjobs, straight-up fucking, no head games. That's what you'll get with me. You can read your books and spend your day as you like. Even take yoga classes. Do we have a deal?"

"Yes, I suppose," I say, trying to back away.

"Good. Take your clothes off and lie on my bed."

This is a more significant test of my loyalty than anything Cruz could concoct. I turn away from Bones, remove my clothing, and fold it carefully, not wanting him to see the listening device inside my shirt or have it shake loose.

"You don't know how long I've waited to put my hands on you," Bones says, sitting on the side of the bed, stroking my arm and moving towards my breasts. "From the first time I saw you, I wanted you." He stops when he sees the ring. "What's this?"

"Just a necklace," I say.

"It looks familiar, but I don't remember where I've seen..." He lets go of it and watches my face. "Hearing you next door with Cruz has been difficult."

He brings his lips to mine. My stomach heaves as Bones thrusts his tongue into my mouth. *Where is Cruz?*

"Stand and face the bed. I'll take you from behind," Bones whispers,

Beep, beep, beep.

"Shit, sorry," Bones says, reaching for his cell. *Pause.* "I'll be there shortly." He shoves the phone in his pocket. "Fuck!" He hits a picture of a dragon hanging on the wall. "I apologize. I have to go," he says, rubbing his hand. "We can resume when I get back."

Bones puts his shirt back on, zipping his pants as he smiles at me, and laces his shoes.

CRUZ

River did everything artfully, as I'd rehearsed with her. During our conversation, she asked me how far she had to go with Bones. "Only do what you're comfortable with," I said. "We'll learn more if he trusts you."

River lowered her head, resigned, like I did when I pretended with Gloria. When River confessed to hearing voices, my mind had to consider the possibility that she suffers from mental illness, not just depression. She could be delusional, like Gloria turned out to be, and for now, I can't trust her, not after Gloria's voices told her to kill me. I push my anger away; it's not River's fault if she has a mental problem. It's Bones I'm angry at.

If I go in before she's done and kill Bones, I might never learn who's behind this: River's husband Jack, Angelo, or someone else. You don't become a successful broker of women without push-back. There's always someone waiting to take your territory, your women, or something else. *What would Gloria have done?*

Most likely, she'd let it play out. Let Bones have River, and spring into action when he's balls deep in her. Drag him off and torture him. Starting with cuts to his dick until she severed his cock, and Bones bled out. Before he died, he would have told her everything worth telling. The problem is that River is in there, and I...

I stop myself. "Love doesn't exist," Gloria said more than once. "Just lust and sex and who's going to fuck who. Do you want to be fucked, little boy?" *No, I did not.* One of the reasons she's gone. I'd watched my mother get fucked over and over by thousands of johns. After they were done with her, they threw her away. She was nothing but skin and bones when she died, and Gloria took me in. When I was old enough, I became her slave and enforcer. I dropped the girls off at appointments and punished them if Gloria believed they'd underperformed or stolen from her. I hardened myself to their tears.

My loyalty to Gloria was absolute. Until she turned on me. "Time to move on, boy," she said. "You're old enough to become someone else's slave." She wouldn't listen, threatening me until I had no choice. I'd learned everything from Gloria that I could. She always said, "The biggest danger in your house is the one you trust and let near you." Gloria had trusted me and paid the price. I'd trusted Bones, and he...

The bed squeaks, and Bones' muffled words from next door come through the speaker. No. *He can't have her*. I grab the knife and head to the doorway when suddenly Bones' phone rings. I stop and listen to the squeak of the bed again, and Bones mumbling. A few minutes later, the slam of Bones' door and footsteps in the hall. His leaving saves his life.

18

KARMA'S A TOUGH TEACHER

CRUZ

"He didn't hurt you, did he?" I ask as I sit in the chair, running my hand over the red velvet cushion. "I'm sorry for sending you in there, and for Angelo too."

River's clothes are disheveled. She crawls into my lap, wraps her arms around me, and burrows her head into my neck. Her body shakes. I stroke her back, attempting to calm her and bring her back to me.

"What do you mean?" she says, trembling. "We needed information from Bones."

"True, but Angelo was a mistake. I thought you'd say no and walk away if I hurt you and—"

"I knew what you were doing, humiliating me on purpose."

"I wanted you to leave, to say no. I'm not used to feeling, and you made me—"

"If you had followed through with Angelo, I would've left. I can't stay with someone ever again if they hurt me on purpose.

I've had a marriage full of that already. I have Alex and Joy to care for, and I have to set a healthy example for them." She pauses. "Did you hear what you needed to from Bones?"

"Yes. Bones is a traitor. I'm happy to learn this. When he returns, I'll deal with him."

"What will you do?"

"Kill him after he tells me who's helping him."

"Isn't there another way?"

"He has your son and daughter, and he's betrayed me. You need to leave. I'll reserve a hotel room for you until I get them back. I don't want you hurt or for you to see any of this."

"I can't leave you to fight alone."

"You're not my slave anymore. I hereby end the contract," I say.

"I'm not leaving. You don't know how many are coming. I'm staying with you." She touches my chest. "I'm not running this time."

***

I survey my room. The last time they'd come through the children's window. As I circle the room, I notice the window in my bathroom is unlocked again. Likely, this is the way they plan to come at me. I go on rounds and realize everyone in the house is gone. This rarely happens. It's only River and me.

We sit in the dark and wait. An hour later, I hear thumping sounds on the lower level. Usually, I can watch everything with my security cameras, but now they're black. More noise comes from the floor below. I'd expected a stealth attack from the bedroom window, but it isn't going down this way. Footsteps and the sounds of someone falling into the wall, perhaps?

"It's her, the ghost," River says as she clings to me. With more thumps, something crashes, forcing my door open. I flip the light switch, and Bones' white face appears in front of me. He is not a ghost, but he looks like one. Something isn't right. He holds the side of his body, stoops over, and suddenly loses his balance, clinging to the wall, leaving bloody handprints behind as he slides down and lands on the floor. I move closer. He lies on his back, his shirt bloody and torn.

"What happened?" I ask, crouching next to him.

"Gia," Bones says, coughing. Then Bones closes his eyes, and his skin turns grey before my eyes.

I search his body. Bones has two large gashes on his stomach. I find River's old phone inside his jacket and another in his pants pocket.

"How did he know my password?" River asks, unlocking her phone and passing it back to me.

"He used to work in the tech industry. I'm sure breaking into your phone wouldn't be a problem." I scan the recent activity. "There are messages from Bones to your husband and a couple of others between Gia and Bones," *Why Gia?*

"Why would Gia help Bones?" River asks, reading my thoughts. "You treated her well."

"True. Come on." I motion to River, leading her to Gia's room. I searched for anything that might explain what Gia was planning on doing and why. I empty her drawers and look under the mattress, but find nothing.

River points to the floor. "There, in front of her bed. One plank seems oddly higher than the others, see? It's leaving a shadow on one side."

I loosen the wood, and the plank comes up. Inside the floor, there's a pad of paper with a to-do list written on it: *wireless speakers; playlist of scary sounds; Bluetooth phone; bottle of des roses.* The same perfume Gloria used to wear. There's a pile of letters as well. I pull one loose, the papers stained and faded. I'd recognize Gloria's handwriting anywhere. I read it aloud.

Gia,

I'm sorry you can't stay with me, but you're old enough to know now my business is not conducive to raising a child. Private schools will give you the education you need. When the time's right, I'll send for you and further your education.

Love, Mother

The others never knew where Gloria went. As time passed, the older ones retired, and new girls took their place. Eventually, none of them even knew of her existence. I'd erased Gloria from the house's collective memory, but not from mine. Gia must have come looking for her mother and suspected me of being responsible for Gloria's disappearance. She can't know for sure. I throw the letters and cards on the floor, and a photo shakes loose, an old picture of Gloria. I look closer and see the baroque pearl necklace around her neck. *Shit.*

River studies the picture, too. "My necklace," she says. "Oh my God, it's the ghost!" she screams, backing away.

"Calm down. It's okay," I say, holding River in my arms.

"You don't understand. It's her, the woman who smells like roses," River says. "Gia asked me where I got the necklace when she did my makeup the other night, too."

Gia knows.

"I can't do this," River says. "Fighting my husband and Bones, I can understand, but I can't hurt Gia. She's been nice to me."

"Don't you get it?" I walk towards her. "She's probably helping your husband and has your children. She sold you out and me, too."

"But why? Why would she?"

"Money, of course, and revenge. She wants me dead." I point at my chest with my thumb.

"But why does she want to kill you?"

"Because I removed someone she loved." *I have to tell River the truth.*

"What do you mean?"

"I killed her mother, Gloria, the woman in the picture."

River backs away, her eyes widening, becoming speechless for several seconds. She stutters, "W-w-when? Why?"

"Years ago, her mother, Gloria, ran The Palace. At one time, my mother worked for her, and when she died, Gloria took me in and said I would be under her care. But it was a lie. She had a plan. She was a monster. When I got old enough, she made me her slave. I had no choice. Several years later, she sold me to someone else. If I didn't go along with it, she threatened to throw me out. I'd lose my job, my home, everything. Gloria and the girls were my only family." I throw my hands out wide.

River's shoulders slump, and a tear rolls down her cheek. "I'm sorry that happened to you," she says, taking small steps toward me. "But maybe you could have gone somewhere and asked for help."

"The cops knew what was going on," Cruz says, rubbing his eyes. "Just like here, how I pay them to turn the other way, and they ignore anything anyone reports. What would they do about it, anyway, when I agreed to become her slave in the first place? I don't regret killing her."

"That's why she's haunting me. She died violently, and she wants you to die too. She told me to kill you. But since I've worn the skull-butterfly around my neck, I don't hear or see her anymore."

"I don't want to disappoint you, but I don't think it's any ghost." I move through the room. I go to the vents over the bed and remove the covers. Behind them, I find the wireless speakers.

"Gia's been playing the voices you've been hearing. Using her phone and sending things through it." I point to the vents. "And the perfume you smelled. She's been spraying it through the heating system."

River wipes her brow and pushes her hair behind her ear. "How do you explain the visions in the mirror and the opening doors and windows?"

"I can't yet, but I'm sure she's got a trick for those, too."

"Maybe you can reason with Gia, explain what happened with her mother, and she'll understand."

"I doubt it. People create fantasies about their family. I'm sure Gia has one for a mother who never really existed. She doesn't realize family always disappoints you in the end."

"Not all families. Families don't have to be your blood. They can be people who love you, stand by your side, whether you do right or wrong, and don't give up on you. Let me try to reason with Gia. You helped her, right? Gave her a place to live and treated her well?"

"I'm her pimp, River. I facilitate her selling herself, and before that, she was... I'm not her psychologist."

"What was she before?"

"My slave, like you," I confess. "How could this happen? I was her mother's slave, and her daughter became mine."

"For how long?"

"She was my slave for four months before I tired of her. I told her she could work here, and she agreed."

"She came to you in the beginning and asked to work here, correct?" River asks.

"Yes."

"Maybe she did all this to get closer to you to find out about her mother. Tell her the truth. Remind her of how well you've treated her and everyone else. Maybe she'll understand why you had to do it."

"Are you not listening? It isn't true. I *haven't* treated everyone well. You, for instance. There might not be any time to explain, anyway. Whoever comes to kill me will probably show up early in the morning. You should leave. Too much could go wrong. Something could happen to you if you're in this room with me."

"I've told you already, I'm not leaving you alone."

"Why? To keep me from killing again? To protect Gia?" I ask, turning away from her.

"No, because you're my family now." She wraps her arms around me, "I want to protect you."

I want to believe River. I need to believe her.

19

IRONY

CRUZ

Abreeze of cold air comes from the bathroom, and there's a slight movement by the lavatory door at two a.m., then I hear slow steps towards the bed. I see a silhouette shape as they creep toward it. I, however, am sitting on the throne with River crouching behind me, waiting for them to make their move. There's a blast of orange light and another towards the bed. They fire seven more times until only the click of an empty gun remains.

I move behind them and hold the knife to their throat. The person doesn't move as my blade touches their skin. The gun slips from their hand and clunks to the floor. "Get the light, River."

When I can see the person's identity, I lower the knife from their throat. "You?"

"Who did you expect?" Gia asks, her eyes wide with the whites showing, her head covered with a red wig. How did I never notice the resemblance to Gloria before now?

River runs towards her. "Where's Alex and Joy? Did you give them to my husband?"

"That was Bones' plan. I had one of my own," Gia says. "Alex and Joy are the family I never had. Cruz stole mine away from me." She points at me.

"You tried to kill me, too," River says, surveying her pillow on the bed, shot full of holes.

"Collateral damage. If I didn't take you out of the picture, you'd never let me keep them," Gia says.

"Where's my husband?" River asks.

Gia snickers. "I did him first. An evil man, like him," she says, pointing at me again.

"He's not," River says, defending me.

"Open your eyes. He'll use you, and in time, down will become up. He made my mother disappear and took my inheritance, too." Gia jabs her finger into my chest. "I was his slave too, like you. He uses people."

"What are you talking about?" I argue. "You begged me to become a slave. You said it would strengthen you, and it did."

"You worked for my mother and betrayed her, and made her change her will," Gia says.

"Yes, I worked for Gloria, but I never even knew she had a will until I found the papers in her safe. It was just as much a surprise to me that she left everything to me. She mentioned a daughter in her diaries, but I couldn't locate you. I didn't know who you were."

"*Liar!* You won't even look at me! What did you do with her?"

"As I said, I didn't know until now that you were her daughter. Money's no problem. I'll share everything with you, on one condition."

"I'm not making a deal with the devil."

"Your mother was the devil. You didn't know her."

"You monster!" she cries, attacking me with her fists as I beat her back and push her into a chair.

"Sit. I'm going to show you this mother of yours." I go to my safe, remove some of Gloria's diaries, and place them on the desk in front of her. "She kept one for every year of her life. I've kept most of them. If I'm ever filled with regret, I take one out and read. Abracadabra, my guilt disappears. Read. When you're finished, if you still want to know the details about her death, I'll tell you."

Gia picks one from the pile and opens it. Her eyes travel the page, glaze over, and she whimpers. At other times, her eyes grow wide.

"I don't believe this. She couldn't have..." She picks up another one and reads some of that, then throws the red-covered book back on the desk. "She didn't even want me. She only got pregnant to blackmail my father. Eventually, she was going to turn me out herself, sell my virginity to the highest bidder, but she didn't have to. I did it to myself, didn't I? What did you do with her?" Gia asks, her eyes softening

"The truth is, I don't know. I gave the body to one of my crew members. He never told me what he did, and I never wanted to know. The guy died of an overdose the following spring."

I return to the safe and remove ten branded stacks of one-hundred-dollar bills, one hundred thousand dollars, and all the boxes of jewelry and gems, and place them in a bag and bring them to the desk. "Here, this is a start. If we get the children back safely, there'll be more. If you don't give us the children, I'm calling the police, and I'm not bluffing."

"I'll take you there."

"You'll tell us where they are, and I'll let you have the cash and the jewelry and arrange for a transfer of some of the properties."

"Happy Holidays Motel, room 222," Gia says.

"Prove it," I say.

"I'll call her son. I left him a burner phone."

"You left him in a room with his dead father?" River screams.

Gia scoffs. "Of course, I didn't. They're in the room next door. Hold on, the phone's ringing." Gia passes the phone to me.

"Hello, Alex," I say. *Pause.* "Yes, it's Cruz. Your mother wants to speak to you." I pass the phone to River. "Gia, take your stuff." I motion to the table. "And then leave."

I watch her take the bag and walk towards the stairs, before turning back. "What about the diaries and the properties?"

"Send a forwarding address, and I'll take care of it."

She nods, and her footsteps echo on the stairs until I hear the door in the vestibule slam.

Six months later

RIVER

"What did the contractor say?" Cruz asks.

"We're lucky to be alive. This new heater is working fine. The heat exchanger on the other one was cracked, but it was more than that. He said some of the vents were blocked. They've installed carbon monoxide detectors in every room."

"I still can't believe it was flooding the house and poisoning us."

"Your bedroom, the cellar, and the great room were the worst, the contractor said.

"As I said, I smelled nothing," Cruz says.

"Of course. It's odorless, colorless, and tasteless. He said it was likely causing my headaches and hallucinations."

"It didn't bother me too much."

"Really? I think it did. It made you mean, and you always complained of headaches. Of course, it may have bothered you worse if you slept in the room all the time."

"Mean? I'm a happy-go-lucky fellow."

"What?" I laugh. "No, you aren't. You're moody, and rigid too. Just a reminder, but my contract ends in one month."

"But I want you here," Cruz says, his nostrils flaring.

"I understand, but my children come first, and we're not from the same worlds."

"Funny, you seem pretty damn into my world when you're stretched across my lap with my hand falling on your ass. You should appreciate my efforts on your behalf. I got your children back."

"*We* got the children back. I fulfilled my end of the bargain." *I love Cruz, but it doesn't mean we can stay together.*

"I don't agree. You haven't fulfilled the contract at all. You talk back, never call me Master, and that's just a start. I need an extension to whip you into shape."

"Ha! Well, when you say it all romantic like that." I laugh. "If I'm so inadequate a slave, why do you want me to stay?"

"Because I want to make it right and turn you into a better one. I can't believe you're still planning on leaving." Cruz's shoulders drop, and he falls into his throne.

"Ahh, no. ...Yes."

"Which one, River?" He reaches out to grip my hand.

"I have to leave. Alex and Joy can't live here, with what goes on in this house. They're getting older. They're going to figure things out. I think Alex is already starting to put some of the pieces together."

"Fine, you win, have it your way," Cruz says in a dismissive tone, waving his hand at me.

Something's very wrong. Cruz never gives up on an argument

because he never accepts no for an answer. This is too easy. "So, you won't try to stop me?" I ask.

"I don't need to. You'll stop yourself. You love me and need what I can provide, slave. What was your orgasm count before you met me? I believe it was two. What's your orgasm count now?" he asks, touching his fingertips together, making a steeple, and bringing them to his chin, a grin spreading. "I'm sure you've lost count by now."

"You sure do think a lot of yourself, don't you?" I smirk.

"I do, but I think even more of you. Consider this: you're the only woman I've ever promised anything to. Or ever apologized to, for that matter. I care for you—"

"Are you attempting to say you love me?" I ask, a smile on my face.

"Yes," Cruz says. "Now, say it back and sign the slave contract renewal."

"Not without negotiation. And you have to say the right words, not make me say them for you."

He gets a stymied look on his face. "Should I get on my knees too?" he asks.

"Great idea."

Cruz lowers himself to the floor. "While I'm groveling down here, I might as well ask you a question."

"I think I require it in writing," I smile.

"It's only one question. Will you marry me?"

"Where's the ring?" I ask.

Cruz reaches up, grabbing the talisman, the blackened skull-butterfly ring hanging around my neck. "I already gave it to you," he says, moving it towards my finger.

PLEASE RATE THIS BOOK

EPILOGUE, ONE YEAR LATER

RIVER

I grab his ass, dig my nails in, and pull him into me. "I'm in charge, not you," Cruz says, pulling back.

"Still with the orgasm denial?" I ask.

"Be quiet, slave." He pushes me away, flipping me on my stomach and hits my backside, the slap echoing through the room. The sting brings a yelp, and my pussy instantly becomes wetter. I'm resting on my forearms, and the tip of his cock parts the lips of my vagina. I'm stretched around him, my body attempting to bring him closer. I try to push back, fuck him, and he slaps me again. "Behave yourself, slave. I drive this train," He brings himself back out, frustrating me. I buck into him again, and he slaps my ass again. "Stop it," he says. "You're squeezing me, trying to make me cum."

"No, I'm trying to make *me* cum," I say.

He laughs and comes back at me, thrusting his cock roughly inside. "Open your legs wider. Do you want it harder or slower?"

"You're giving me a choice, or is this a trick question?"

"I don't need tricks for you to cum on my cock. All I have to do is say the words, and you'll come apart. Should I say them, River, or make you wait another day or two?" My pussy clenches around his cock, and he grinds into me harder, giving me all of him. "Either you stop, or I do," he says, "because if you keep doing that, I'm going to—"

I buck into him, my pussy clenching around him.

"I can't hold back anymore," he says, and he brings his lips to my ear, "Don't forget when you climax, think of... something sweet, River. Cum. Now."

My pussy pulls him in tighter, let's go, and tightens again, over and over. I try to push him away, the intensity too much, but he doesn't let me.

"Keep going. Make it last," he says as he brings my hips towards him, continuing to ram into me from behind. "Good girl," he says as my orgasm tapers off and his begins. "My turn," he says. "I can't last any longer, your pussy's getting too strong, even for me." He pumps faster, and then suddenly his cock spasms, and he spills his fire into me. Our bodies and fluids join, and he presses down onto my back. I feel all his weight, making me feel safe under him. The scent of sex is everywhere.

"Good afternoon," Cruz growls in his throaty voice in my ear, licking my neck and biting it, coming in for a sideways kiss. "I love you, slave."

A door slams, and we both stop like deer frozen in headlights. Cruz pops up from the bed and looks out the window. "Shit, the kids are home," he says.

"They're home early," I say, scrambling off the bed and reaching for my clothes.

CRUZ

"What have you decided?" River asks.

"I can't sell The Palace. It's the only home I've ever known," I say.

"Are you sure about this? I love the place too, but how can we maintain it? It's a mausoleum. How can we fill all this space now that everyone's moved out?"

"Do what you said, foster children, help runaways. And actually, it's an old church, not a mausoleum."

"Are the girls coming over this weekend?"

"Yes, they'll celebrate the winter solstice with us. Everyone's bringing a dish for the celebration."

"I got a phone call from the attorney," River says. "Jack's estate will settle by the end of the year, now that they've finally received the police report, drug deal gone bad. I'm going to put it all in a trust fund for the children."

"Yeah, I made sure that was the conclusion they'd reach," I say. Planting money, the drugs, and Bones' handless body kept the heat off Gia and us. They had no way to identify Bones.

"One of my husband's partners was trying to hold up the will, but he didn't have cause."

"Who was he?" I ask.

"Some Russian guy."

"You should throw him a bone."

"I'll talk to the attorney about it."

"As soon as this settles, we need to set a date. I never thought I'd have the opportunity, but I want to be Joy and Alex's father."

"You aren't losing your focus on me, are you?" she asks, smiling, her eyes lighting up.

"I got you to sign a renewal slave contract after a vicious negotiation, so what do you think?"

"True, but I got it down to one page, and you had to make concessions."

"I've strengthened you. You're not afraid of anyone anymore. Even me. Although you're still sweet and gentle," I stroke her head. Her hair is growing back.

"You've changed, too, Cruz. You don't make people suffer anymore. Well, only in the best way, inside the bedroom."

"I'm connecting you with your female energy, your magic."

"Thank you. And I'm giving you something too, something to live for—a family," River says. She clasps my hand and pulls me in front of our altar, and we pray.

Buzz, buzz. "Let it go," she says as I look at my phone. A text from Angelo:

> It's time for me to collect.

"WHO IS IT?" she asks.

"Just business stuff," I mutter, shoving the phone deep in my pocket, hoping the problem will go away. But since this is his third text in the past couple of days, it's unlikely.

THE END

PLEASE RATE THIS BOOK

· · ·

Read the next book in the series, The Devil I Love

OTHER BOOKS BY KAY FREEMAN

Or Purchase More Directly From Kay

Contemporary Gothic Romance:

Leather Man

The Devil Chronicles Series:

The Devil I Love

The Devil I Fear

Suspense Romance:

Truth Moon, by Wild Rose Publishing

Hitman's Heart Series:

Hitman's Honey

Hitman's Holiday

Hitman's Honeymoon

The Flower Queen Series:

The Flower Queen

Seeds of Justice

Contemporary Gothic, Paranormal:

Other Worlds

Audiobooks also available for various titles.

Visit Kay's website to learn more: https://www.kaylaafreeman.com/

About Kay

Kay Freeman spent the early part of her career as a professional artist. She's shown her work throughout the United States under her professional name, Kay A. Klotzbach. Kay was a full-time art professor in South Jersey for over 23 years and was awarded a Princeton Mid-Career Fellowship for her teaching and community-based service-learning projects.

Kay decided to pursue her passion for writing after her manuscript, *Truth Moon*, was selected by Romance Writers of America's RAMP program in 2021, which led to its publication as her debut novel by The Wild Rose Press. Kay has since self-published nine other novels.

Kay has won several awards for her writing. In 2022, Hitman's Honey won third place in the Mid Atlantic Author Society's Romance Contest, and in 2024, her novel *Leather Man* was a finalist in Passionate Ink's Passionate Plume Contemporary Short Category. Her novel *The Flower Queen* topped Amazon's Best Seller List in June 2023 in the Historical Romance 20th Century category. In 2025, her novel *Other Worlds* won a Stiletto in the speculative category. Kay is celebrated for crafting hard-won happily-ever-afters that involve spiritual journeys and transformations for her characters.

For the past four years, she has also written a publication for romance authors, *What Do Romance Authors Think About,* a free Substack newsletter to give back to those who have helped her.

Besides her passion for art, reading, and writing, she loves the blues, tequila, baking bread, and her husband, Barry. Kay lives in Wilmington, DE. You can learn more and sign up for her newsletter for readers on KaylaaFreeman.com.

www.ingramcontent.com/pod-product-compliance
Lightning Source LLC
Chambersburg PA
CBHW070831160726
48004CB00001B/331